Alamo. It somehow combined the fanciful, what-if philosophy of 'The Last Temptation of Christ' with the delicious possibilities presented in the best episodes of 'Meeting of Minds' or Steve Martin's wonderful play, 'Picasso at the Lapin Agile'. I recommend this book to anyone interested in American history, but more importantly, to anyone who enjoys a chance to listen in on what might have transpired between great men with great thoughts had they had the opportunity to really get into each other's heads." -- Adrienne Armstrong, **co-author, *Backstage with the Original Hollywood Square*** (w/ Peter Marshall, Rutledge Hill Press)

Cover design/artwork by Fletcher Rhoden.

Order this book online at www.trafford.com/07-2958
or email orders@trafford.com

Most Trafford titles are also available at major online book retailers.

Note for Librarians: A cataloguing record for this book is available from Library and Archives Canada at www.collectionscanada.ca/amicus/index-e.html

ISBN: 978-1-4251-5265-9

www.trafford.com

North America & international
toll-free: 1 888 232 4444 (USA & Canada)
phone: 250 383 6864 • fax: 250 383 6804
email: info@trafford.com

The United Kingdom & Europe
phone: +44 (0)1865 722 113 • local rate: 0845 230 9601
facsimile: +44 (0)1865 722 868 • email: info.uk@trafford.com

10 9 8 7 6 5 4

Critical acclaim for *Last Tango With Marlon*, a stage play in two acts written and directed by Fletcher Rhoden

"Fletcher Rhoden has written a fascinating play about the unlikely friendship between Wally Cox and Marlon Brando, and it is fast moving and full of interesting tidbits. Veteran actors Frank Cavestani as Marlon, and Raf Mauro as Wally... make it work. There is Frank as a heavy Marlon, complete with his familiar high-pitched and halting delivery, and then there is Raf as the short, bespectacled Wally, who is intensely comedic. Rhoden's meticulous research gives the audience insight into their relationship. In addition to directing, [Rhoden] handled the sound effects like a pro." -- **The Tolucan Times, Feb. 6, 2008**

"Though not obscure, Wally Cox is certainly less well remembered than his childhood friend and perennial buddy, Marlon Brando. In Fletcher Rhoden's new play, set in Brando's study in 1974, Cox returns from the grave to visit his aging friend... The dialogue is leavened with duets, fake football games and the kind of horseplay they indulged in as kids. The play is brightened by the deliciously funny Raf Mauro as Cox, who, with exquisite comic timing, makes us understand why Brando hated to see him go." -- **CurtainUp.com, Feb. 4, 2008**

"A funny and touching play. Written by Fletcher Rhoden, who knew more than a few of those Hollywood Squares as a kid, and draws from some of that too. Raf Mauro as the ghost of Wally Cox is a constant delight." -- **Mayor Sam's Sister City, blogspot.com Feb. 2008**

Critical acclaim for *The Trial Of Davy Crockett*, a novella by Fletcher Rhoden, available from Trafford Publishing

"**The Trial Of Davy Crockett** is a speculative fiction novella. Author Fletcher Rhoden questions whether Davy Crockett was truly killed during the battle for the Alamo -- or whether he was captured and executed by the Mexicans. **The Trial Of Davy Crockett** presents a hypothetical dialogue between Crockett and *Generalissimo* Antonio López de Santa Anna, who collide in an articulate, wry, thought-provoking, and no-holds-barred verbal conflict regarding the Texian Revolution and America's unrestrained expansionism. Neither Crockett or Santa Anna is stereotyped in the roles of hero or villain; their opposing points of view are given a clear and fair hearing, for all to see and judge for themselves. Based entirely on the facts of the revolution, **The Trial Of Davy Crockett** is a 'must' for Texas history buffs and not to be missed." -- **The Midwest Book Review, November 11, 2001**

"One of the obscure facts about the famous stand at the Alamo during the Texas war for liberation from Mexico is that Davy Crockett and a handful of others were captured alive by Santa Anna's forces when the mission-turned-fort fell. He and the others were summarily executed soon afterwards. Fletcher Rhoden has carefully crafted a novella that is based on the facts of the Texas revolution that gives fair and equal expression to both sides of the conflict and is thoughtful yet riveting reading from first page to last." -- **The Midwest Book Review's library newsletter, *The Bookwatch*, October 2001**

"I read **The Trial of Davy Crockett** by Fletcher Rhoden last week. From the moment I picked it up I couldn't put it down, and now that I've finished reading it I haven't been able to stop thinking about it. It's an extremely well-written and carefully crafted piece, and the author obviously took great pains with his research. I'm interested in Texas history, but I'm certainly not an aficionado of the genre. What really fascinated me was the humanistic approach that Rhoden took with the meeting of these two larger-than-life historical characters, Davy Crockett and *Generalissimo* Antonio López de Santa Anna, at the battle for the

Last Tango With Marlon

A novella
by
Fletcher Rhoden

For A:

Thanks for the life.

Love,
F.

Chapter One

"I don't give a damn," Marlon Brando shouted into the phone. "I can't play an Indian, they'll never buy it." Then Dennis Banks had to mention *Viva Zapata!* It was one of Marlon's better performances and it was as a Mexican. "That's old news, Dennis. I want *Wounded Knee* to make *Zapata!* look like *Candy*."

Does everybody need everything explained to them all the time? Marlon wondered. *Isn't there anybody who just plain gets it?* Dennis' answer came just as Marlon dreaded it would in the few seconds since he made the reference. "I know you didn't see *Candy*; nobody did, that's my ... Anyway, I can't play Sitting Bull. It'll look like a minstrel show."

Marlon walked past the Victorian walnut nursing chair and sat at the round French center table. "I have to play a rancher or a marshal or something. But I'm not gonna jump around in a headdress like I'm on fucking *F Troop*."

The terrible little itch that'd been roaming his upper back all night returned to compete with the phone call for Marlon's attention. It found a spot under his left shoulder blade, too near the center of his back to be an easy reach. But the buzz in his ear was the more pressing annoyance.

"So talk to the writer," Marlon said. "The audience sympathizes with whomever he decides, if he knows what the hell he's doing." But this was Abby Mann, who'd written *Judgment at Nuremberg*. So he knew what the hell he was doing, Marlon was sure of that.

"I know I recommended him." Marlon said, impatient with Dennis' lack of Marlon's own certainty. "Now I recommend you call him and work it out. You know the history, you know the details. You're the head of the American Indian Movement, not me."

Marlon's skin tingled with mischief as he snaked between the nursing chair and the center table and grabbed Wally Cox's urn from the shelf.

"Hold on," Marlon said into the phone. "I'll have Wally explain it to you."

Marlon lowered the telephone receiver to the urn, the earpiece toward the top and the mouthpiece curving around to the front, as though the urn were a porcelain head. He could almost imagine Wally's voice, big words and bigger ideas in that small, nasal tone. In the echo of Marlon's memory there were traces of Wally's cozy, Middle American logic, his courteous frankness. *Wally could make this guy understand,* Marlon thought.

But the urn said nothing, even as Marlon's imagination raced with every clever retort Wally might offer; every blind alley Wally's intellect might gleefully leap in a single, pithy bound. But the only sound was Dennis' confused request for Marlon leaking up from the telephone receiver.

"Well I can't explain it any better than that," Marlon said, his voice lazy with confidence. But even Wally's impeccable, unspoken logic hadn't convinced Dennis, who made the same suggestion he'd made three times in the past two days. Marlon answered, "No, don't have him call me, I want you two to deal with this. I can't do it all myself, Dennis. I've got Tahiti, the kids, my ex-wife. Every man has his limits. Now will you help me or not?"

The long silence reminded Marlon that Dennis didn't have to help him at all. And Marlon knew that without Dennis Banks and Russell Means, *Wounded Knee* was not likely to get made, at least not by Marlon Brando.

But the lilting tone in Dennis' voice reassured Marlon. Unfortunately, this was just long enough to allow that annoying itch to return to the left side of Marlon's back. His fingers dug at the thickening layer of hairy fat, but his fingernails streaked across the smooth silk robe. He probed under his pajama tops, also silk, but still couldn't find the right spot.

One crisis would have to be dealt with at a time, however, and the nagging itch could wait. Dennis needed a little stroking. He'd said yes, after all. "Good man, Dennis, I really do appreciate your help. Now please conference it out with Abby and I'll check back in a couple days."

He hung up the phone and silence returned to the study. That house in the Hollywood Hills might as well have been on the moon. Not for the first time that day, Marlon wished it was.

But there'd be no easy out. There never had been, despite the false promises of fame and wealth and the warm, open arms of physical pleasure. Those were traps of their own. Every good thing in Marlon's life seemed rigged to spring on him at his most relaxed and snap shut on his spine, his heart, his soul.

Wally's urn stood on the table near the center of the study. One of Wally's favorite sayings, from one of his own books, camc back to Marlon's memory.

"You're right again, Wally," Marlon said as he dropped himself into the chair in front of the urn. "They don't make adults like they used to."

Marlon ran his fingers along the side of the urn, cold and smooth under his fingertips. Then his fingers curled into a fist. Marlon pounded the oak tabletop, the weight of the urn not preventing it from shaking with the blow. The clap of his fist against the table reverberated through the study and, Marlon was quite sure, through the rest of the house.

But it couldn't chase the silence away for long, or the demons that lurked in it; his mistakes, his failures.

He could almost feel them crawling around the study like rats, inching closer, creeping up on him from behind. Marlon's spine shivered with the imagined scratching of their little claws on the wooden floor, feeding on the stacks of old magazines and on his conscience. When he slept, they bit at his toes. When he ate, they gnawed at his genitals. When he drank, they burrowed into his skull.

"Wally, what am I doing wrong? I can't talk to anyone anymore, except you. I feel like I'll never make any real progress. Christian's still drinking. Jesus, he's only a kid. He stole pot from the neighbor's private stash, did I tell you that? One day Jack Nicholson turns up at the door."

Marlon's skills were still sharp enough to recreate that famous drawl and those creeping brows. "Listen, Captain, I got no beef with you. In fact, I was hoping we might make a picture together, kind of like Abbott and Costello or something. But if I find that kid of yours dipping his beak into my weed jar again I'm gonna have him arrested on a B & E, and that's after I break his fucking fingers. Understood?"

Dropping the voice and facial expression with no more thought than he gave to picking them up, Marlon walked to the other side of the room. The bottle of *Courvoisier* was almost full.

"It's his mother's fault," Marlon told the urn, pouring a snifter of cognac. "She's no better'n any of 'em; filthy, lying bitch. But I'm not going to let her poison his mind against me or against life."

The *Courvoisier* streamed up his nostrils before the liquid reached his tongue. It went down hot, a satisfying burn in his throat that melted into a reassuring warmth in his belly and bones.

But one look at the urn turned that warmth into a cold stone in Marlon's gut. "Don't look at me that way, Wally. I'm doin' my God-damned best."

The phone rang, a quick shiver running up Marlon's spine.

He knew it was Anna Kashfi even before raising the phone to his ear. Her voice made his skin crawl. The softness he'd loved about it years before, when she was still Mrs. Marlon Brando, was gone. The subtle sweetness of her coo had evolved into a sharp slap in the face. "Oh, it's you," Marlon said. "I should have recognized the whiff of sulfur when the phone rang."

As soon as Marlon paused, just enough to draw a breath, she launched her attack. She'd done it before and, Marlon was certain, she would keep doing it. He had long since decided, *Why pretend to acquiesce?*

"That's right," Marlon said. "I'm taking him to Tahiti, getting him out of this cesspool and away from those shit heels who are slowly killing him."

She assumed he included her in that group. When she confirmed it, Marlon could only say, "If the shit heel fits, honey."

Then she went on about her lawyers, the threats of the courts and all the other crap she used to cut Marlon off from his darling firstborn. She might as well have been using them to strangle the life right out of him, and out of Christian too.

"Your lawyers, is that so?" Marlon started leafing through an imagined file cabinet. He knew she couldn't see, but it was more for his own amusement. "Okay, hold on a sec: I ... I Did ... I Don't ... I Don't Gossip, oops, too far ... I Don't Give ... here it is, I Don't Give A Shit." He dropped an imaginary file into the imaginary drawer and shut it. "All filed away, you psychotic whore."

She rushed through a few final threats and insults before what Marlon knew would be the slamming of the phone.

"Don't you hang up on me. I'm not finished with you, not by a long shot." But the click of the phone and the steady buzz of the dial tone told Marlon that Anna was finished with him, at least for the night.

Finished, Marlon thought to himself.

"See what I mean?" Marlon said rhetorically to Wally's urn as he crossed to the Regency Gillows of Lancaster writing table. "How much more can I do?"

The .357 Magnum seemed heavier than its mere two pounds,

nickel plating catching the glare of the light. It was cold in his sweating palm, the polished walnut handle slipping under his nervous fingers. "I know what you're thinking, Wally. *This again?* Well, this'll be the last time, I promise. I'm tired, Wally, I'm so sick and tired of all this bullshit."

The distance from the desk to the center table seemed impossibly long, his destination inching out ahead of him as if forever beyond his reach. Marlon stopped near the love seat and leaned against it, knowing he'd soon have to muster more strength than he'd produced in some time, perhaps his entire life; and all in one great, albeit final, burst.

"I got nothin' left," Marlon muttered, the words both frightening and seducing him. "Not for the pictures, my family. They'd be better off without me, truth be told; Christian especially."

When he heard himself say it, voice so close to his own ear, he knew it for what it was; the truth.

And a death sentence.

Not expecting or even wanting an answer, Marlon asked, "So what the fuck am I hanging around for?"

No answer came. Marlon's arm lacked the conviction to raise the gun to his chin. Instead it showed him the weapon, offering him a last chance to back out and save himself.

Or convict himself beyond any reasonable doubt.

"I should have died back in the day, like James Dean, forever young and beautiful. You knew the score, right, Wally? When to bow out gracefully."

There were still so many doubts, so many unanswered questions. But Marlon was flush with the idea that he'd have a chance to ask Wally in person after only a few moments.

"No such thing as natural causes," Marlon said with a shake of his head. "Not for people like us."

Anger swelled in Marlon's chest, indignation and a martyr's fury. With his free hand, he reached out for the phone. His fingers clamped around the receiver as if to squeeze it to death. Marlon rose it to his face so fast he nearly broke a tooth.

"You hear that?" he screamed into the phone. "You win, you bitch! Hear me? You fucking win!"

He slammed the phone down, turning to an audience of none; not even Wally.

Do it, a little voice said in the back of Marlon's ear. *Do it, you coward. Pull the trigger.*

Marlon could almost recognize the voice but his doomed, drunken will refused him the opportunity. The gun felt lighter, rising with a strange effortlessness in his certain grip. The gun had stopped shaking, nerves quieted by reckless certainty. The muzzle was colder than he expected against his double chin. Marlon flinched, but his index finger would not be so easily startled as it mounted the trigger and prepared to squeeze.

Marlon's heart slowed, resolved to its fate. His lungs surrendered, taking those last few breaths with shocking timidity. They were tired too. His whole God-damned body was tired.

Here it is, Brando, Marlon told himself. *Any last words?* His mind raced across a sea of quotes and phrases, thoughts and images rolling in the moonlight of his recollection. *How do you say goodbye to life itself?*

He thought of Wally, of the heroes and misfits they loved and were. "What was that line from *Cyrano*?" After a moment to reflect, the words crawled over Marlon's shocked tongue. "And then as I end the refrain -- "

"Thrust home!" The voice was as sharp and real in Marlon's ear as the last time he heard it; thin and small, a steady monotone tucked into the back of the throat just under the nasal cavity. The slight lisp on *thrust* left no room for doubt.

Wally.

"Hello, Bud."

Chapter Two

No, Marlon reminded himself, *it can't be.* Yet there he stood, broad shoulders drooping in that same wrinkled, brown suit. His thin mustache was graying, like the temples of his receding hairline. Another gulp of cognac made Wally all the more realistic.

The feet turned to inches, Wally reaching out in their familiar childhood salute. Wally touched Marlon's nose with the tip of his index finger and held it there. Marlon did the same to Wally's nose.

Marlon said, "Needles."

"Pins," Wally countered.

"Triplets."

"Twins."

"When a man marries -- "

"The trouble begins."

"When a man dies -- "

"His troubles will end." Wally removed his index finger from Marlon's nose and Marlon removed his from Wally's. But as their hands crossed, their pinkies interlocked.

Marlon asked, "What goes up the chimney?"

"Smoke."

Together, they said, "The promise between us will never be broke."

Each closed his eyes. Marlon's inner voice muttered his wish, in the darkness of his imagination Wally did the same. He opened his eyes just as Wally did, squinting in the light. But there was one more gesture to complete the ritual greeting. Marlon's thumb stood tall, pressing against Wally's for a few seconds. Together, Marlon and Wally said, "Thumbs," before their digits slipped off with a slight twist.

This fixed things in Marlon's mind; Wally was back. A flood of warmth welled up in Marlon. His skin tingled, breath easy in his lungs. The corners of his smile pressed into his sagging jowls. His thickening face wrinkled up at the corners of his eyes.

They hugged. Marlon patted Wally's back, firm and broad under that baggy suit, to assure himself that this unusual visit was more than just his drunken imagination. And if not, the sheer force of his will would make it so. No mere law of the physical world would prevent this happy reunion.

"I've missed you, Wally, I can hardly say."

But before Wally could return the compliment, Marlon lunged at him.

"Killer Brando gets Cox in a headlock," Marlon said, at once the beastly Killer and the rapid-talking announcer calling the action. Wally's head peeked out of Marlon's armpit. Marlon could almost feel Wally's palms pressing against his back, then his little friend's fingers pulling at his left arm. In Marlon's ears a stadium of fans cheered and booed, the full froth of a championship bout. "There's no love loss between these two titans of the ring," Marlon's announcer went on, "but only one can emerge victorious. Can the baby face get loose?"

Wally struggled, balance shifting as he tried to yank free.

Marlon's announcer declared, "Wily Wally Cox has had it, folks. What an end to such a sterling and fabled career; three-year world champion, a hero to children everywhere. And it's all over, folks. Yes, it looks like a finish ..."

Wally pulled out of the hold, slipping past Marlon's fading muscles. He grabbed Marlon's vulnerable right wrist and yanked it back almost to his left shoulder blade. "Oh, Cox turns the tables on the Killer," Wally said, doing his own announcer's voice. "The crowd goes wild!"

Wally reached around Marlon's neck with his left arm, pulling him back. Marlon could almost feel his throat being choked off, muscles straining against Wally's forearm.

"An incredible turnabout," Wally's announcer said. "The underdog has the giant dead to rights. Will the Killer tap out?"

Marlon reached for the table, but Wally had him bent backward. In his wrestler's voice, Marlon said, "I'll never tap out," and then after a slight pause, "I can't reach!"

Wally let go, Marlon fell forward and his flat palm smacked against the tabletop. His ass hit the chair a second later.

"Cox wins the day!" Wally threw up his hands and the crowd leapt to their feet. Their cheers receded into Marlon's inner ear.

"Christ it's good to see you, Wally. How've you been?"

"Well, Bud, I am dead for over a year now, so I guess you could say things have been better." With a wry look down at the floor and beyond, he added, "Then again, things could be a whole lot worse."

"I knew you'd make it in, Wally. But you're still wearing that same crappy suit."

Wally shrugged. "It's heaven, they'd want you to be comfortable. Can you imagine? Everywhere you look it's bunny slippers and old bathrobes and *La-Z-Boy* recliners."

Marlon *could* imagine it, a cloudy haven of nerds and good-natured slobs lolling eternity away in complete contentment. Marlon asked, "Cognac?" Wally shook his head. "Sandwich? Isn't there something I can get you, anything I can do?"

"I thought maybe there was something I could do for you."

"Me? *Nah.* Things were a little rough goin' for a while, I admit; not just the pictures, I mean. But everything's coming together now. With *Godfather* and *Tango* I'm on top again. I can handle it."

Wally picked up the Magnum, holding it with the tips of his thumb and middle finger, his pinky extended. He glared at Marlon as he returned the revolver to the writing table on the other side of the room.

"Everybody needs a little help sometimes, Bud."

There was no arguing the point. Wally was right. And Marlon was glad for the help and thrilled with the company, even if he was more enthused about the company than the help. He leaned back, pinching the ridge of his nose between the eyes.

"You're right, Dr. Cox. I'm in trouble here, serious trouble." Marlon leaned back further, sensing the smile on Wally's face. "I know it sounds bizarre, but I just can't shake this feeling that I'm ..."

After a long, dramatic pause, Marlon added, " ... A chicken."

Wally pretended to look over a note pad. In a Viennese accent, he asked, "And how long, *zese* feelings you've been having?"

"Since I was an egg. I was never religious, even though my father was a fryer."

But Marlon couldn't relish his own wordplay for long. That tenacious itch skimmed across his back, tracing a subtle burn. "You really wanna be a help?"

Wally nodded, fingers clawed. Marlon could almost feel Wally's scratching nails move with rhythmic precision. Just the suggestion was enough for the time being. It would have to be.

"Hey, Wally, remember back in Evanston?"

"The good ol' days, when a nickel was worth a nickel's worth of joy."

Marlon said, "At Lincoln Elementary," and Wally joined him in the school's unofficial motto.

"Best in the nation!"

"Did you ever think we'd wind up the way we did?" Marlon asked.

"It's not over yet, at least not for you."

Wally stepped into the room, expanding his chest and pushing his muscular shoulders back. He planted his fists on his hips like he was Superman. "I thought I'd be a square-jawed hero who jumped out of airplanes and swung from the trees to catch criminals. I'd rely solely on my amazing physique, my trusty Bowie knife and of course my pet lion, Samson." He lowered his fists, which opened in submission as his shoulders drooped. "Where did I go wrong?"

"That, my old friend, is the question of the day."

"No, the real question is, 'How do you go right?'"

But Marlon pretended not to hear him, or to play it off as though he had no idea what Wally meant. Better to keep the conversation moving in another direction, even if that happened to be backward. "Life was an improvisation. What a pair we made; Wally the wit -- "

"Buddy the bod."

"We were destined to be friends from the time your old man met Dodie in Chicago. Of course, I wasn't sickly like you."

Wally's head tipped on his shoulders as he considered. "Sickly, little Wally. Uh, I guess I may have been prone to the odd cold or two. I did get pretty sick after that game of cowboys when you tied me to a tree. I was there for hours."

The day came roaring back; the gray Illinois sky, the shrieks of the children as their alter egos died from imagined gunshot wounds and flying arrows. Marlon remembered the tree he tied Wally to, the boy's voice as he called out to be released. The voice got softer as it got more distant.

"My father eventually came and untied me." Marlon's stomach turned, guilty nausea stirring his bile. Wally added, "And then there were times I was faking, or I got sick on purpose. To get time off school, of course."

Of course, Marlon reassured himself. *No reason I would have anything to do with that.*

"When you were on your feet, you were a hell of a lawman." Marlon pushed himself up out of the Louis XV side chair. By the time he stood erect he was no longer in his study but in an abandoned lot back in Evanston, decades earlier. And he was transported from Evanston to the dusty streets of Buckeye or Carson City or some other area typical of a young boy's Wild West fantasies. His hands were steady at his hips. Wally assumed a similar posture; legs spread, head forward, arms akimbo, fingers ready to grab for his guns.

"But those days are over," Marlon said, his voice a deadly western twang. "Word's out you gone soft, Sheriff, took to the bottle. Ain't no two-bit, run-down, tinhorn greenhorn gonna bring in ol' Buddy Aberdeen Brando."

Wally's eyes were locked on Marlon's. "Give it up, Aberdeen. We gotcha f'r horse stealin', cattle rustlin', train robbin' ... rapin' a cactus?"

"It was dark." Suddenly Marlon was channeling Jack Benny, with his broad takes and round syllables. "Anyway, I reckon I been punished enough on *that* score, Sheriff."

"Tell it to the judge, Aberdeen. We got the place surrounded. The rest of your gang's either tied up outside or in the pokey."

In Aberdeen's determined hiss, Marlon said, "Then I guess I'll die alone. Unless you'd like to join me."

Marlon drew his guns and fired.

But Wally was quicker. Amid the spit-filled gun noises each man made as he fired, Marlon dropped his imaginary guns and clutched his gut. He fell to his chair, only half on it as he shakily reached for his drink. He took a final swig, still clutching his mortally wounded belly. He swallowed hard and winced, squinting up at Wally. He looked like he was about to speak, to offer some parting wisdom or a last gesture of friendship to his victorious opponent. But a dramatic pain took him in the chest and, with a final grimace, Marlon fell forward.

Wally said, "Nobody could take a fall like you, Bud."

When Marlon opened his eyes he was back in his study, once more the middle-aged screen legend shambling around in his pajamas; drinking and carrying on an imagined conversation with his best friend Wally Cox, dead for over a year.

Everything was back to normal.

Marlon said, "You know the death scene in *Godfather*, with the orange peel and the kid and the tomato plants, that was my idea."

"I knew as soon as I saw it. You were great, Bud, really. Congratulations on getting the award, by the way. I didn't have a chance to say so before."

But Wally didn't mean, *In this conversation before now.* Wally meant, *Before I died.*

There was a handy remedy for this grim reminder in the tantalizing distraction of Sacheen Littlefeather, whom Marlon had sent to decline the award for him in the name of the American Indian. "What did you think of

Littlefeather's speech?"

"Honestly, I thought it would have been more powerful if *you* had delivered the speech, Bud."

Marlon shook his head. "People will be talking for years about the pretty Indian girl getting shouted down by those jerks. What a heroine, what a story. If I'd gone, they'd just be talking about how fat Brando was. Get their attention and hold it, Dodie taught me that. Y'know she used to brew her own beer at home, during prohibition. I'd come home after school and the whole place would smell of hops, just positively reek of this hot, sticky smell." Marlon could taste the doughey stink on the back of his tongue, his nostrils cramping. The feel of the old couch, patches worn through to the foam, the sound of the radio in the living room in the hours after he'd gone to bed; memories bombarded Marlon, too many to decipher. He could only shut them all out and refocus on Wally. Another shot of *Courvoisier* drained the snifter but the bottle wasn't far.

"My mother had a shattered, poetic kind of elegance," was all Marlon could think to say. At least it was true. And this was one truth Marlon was happy to face.

"She was great, I always thought." Wally's words echoed in their humble simplicity. But they were too humble, too simple to describe Dorothy Pennebaker Myers Brando, Marlon's deceased mother.

"Dodie was a healer," Marlon said, pictures of her flashing across his memory.

More images crept up on Marlon, his old demons sniffing at his naked heels. "My father was the authority of the house, when he wasn't traveling or out on a drunken binge of whore mongering. But Dodie was the one who held the family together."

Marlon could see the sadness trace Wally's features, the arc of the eyebrows and the twitch of the mustache. "I'm sorry, Wally, I don't mean to go on about my mother."

"No, it's okay. I always wished I'd had a chance to see her act."

"She was more than an actress, because it was only when she was up on that stage that she was really living. When my father moved the family away from Chicago and she lost the theater, started spending all her time at home; that's when she started to die."

"Similar pattern with my mom. When she left the house, that's when she really started to live. Of course, *she* never came back."

With only the slightest reticence, Marlon asked, "Is it true that you had a picnic on her grave?" Wally nodded. Though Marlon had never broached the subject, this seemed like a reasonable time to say, "But, I mean, what the hell, right? So your mom runs off with another woman?"

"And was a raging drunk."

"So was my mom," Marlon said.

"So are you."

"And so were you!"

"Maybe you should consider my example, Bud, while there's still time."

Marlon reached for the snifter, filling it even higher before taking another gulp to illustrate the extent to which he was willing to consider Wally's advice.

"Well you weren't drunk at nine, were you?" Marlon asked, knowing the answer. He was more interested in changing the subject; and nostalgia was a ready topic for any occasion, especially this one. "Of course that might explain the sickliness. But then how could you have read all those books?"

Wally let a distressed chuckle tumble out of his mouth as he shook his head. "Did it ever interest you that I hated homework, that I read as little as possible? It wasn't my fault that I was able to do as I was told. And anybody can appreciate literature if he puts his mind to it."

"What about all those *Oz* books?"

"Oh, that's different. Oz was a place where the main characters were kids or animals or creatures made of some material other than meat. What kid wouldn't love that? But put a book in the hands of a boy my size ... I was small, obedient, courteous and got good grades; that was more than enough to hang a man."

Marlon winked. "Oz was enough to hang you, Wally."

"But I *loved* to go out and play. During the fall I couldn't wait for the first snow. I would grab my sled, pull on my high-top boots and go outside and stand around waiting for a long, lonely hour. The sled would get wet, I'd catch cold and eventually stumble back to the house. A sled dragged over bare ground makes the saddest sound in the world."

What a picture he could paint, Marlon marveled, able to see the childhood Wally stooped in the gray mist. "It usually took a month of flurries before there was any real snow on the ground, Wally."

"That's right. But every year I'd be out there early, every year I'd be disappointed. I just couldn't learn from my mistakes."

Marlon knew what Wally was getting at and was eager not to follow him to it. And he couldn't shake that Norman Rockwellesque picture of young Wally, sad and sagging in the infant winter. "You were so small and cute, like a hamster."

Wally cringed. "Small, cute, cute, small; horrible, interchangeable words. I loathed that they applied to me. And I still wish I had a penny for every time some large creature called me either of those names. The worst of it was that I was raised to be nice and to smile and all that nonsense. If just once I'd been allowed to say, 'Aw, shut up.'"

"Or, 'Fuck off!'"

"One, I might have grown taller from sheer reduction of hostility and two, I might not have hated performing for as long as I did."

That makes sense, Marlon said to himself. "You never did feel comfortable on stage, did you, Wally?"

Wally reached for the snifter. "Making my debut as a Scottish Highlander in the elementary school follies didn't help. There I was in front of the entire school; cute, small, and wearing a green plaid skirt."

"It's a good thing that fabled phallus of yours didn't pop out, scare half those kids to death; not to mention what it would have done to the other half." Marlon looked over Wally's muscular physique. "And what did you bench, two-twenty?"

"Two-forty. If that kilt had been red, I'd probably have broken three hundred."

But there was more to Wally's childhood than a sad-sack, hard luck sissy with an unnaturally large penis. Marlon was happy to remind Wally, "It wasn't all lollipops and Pickup Sticks with you, sunshine. Who was that girl you used to make fun of, Nasty Vagina?"

"*Virginia,* Nasty Virginia." Wally chuckled, and Marlon wasn't sure if he was amused by his own bullying or by Marlon's new twist on the old moniker. Marlon wanted to believe Wally's imagination took him back to Evanston to call the girl by this new and terrible nickname, and that Wally was returning to the Brando study with the fresh laughter still on his lips. But when the chuckle was replaced with a solemn half smile, Marlon knew he'd guessed wrong.

"We were just being kids, y'know," Wally explained. "But you're right. If you want to feel terrible for thirty years, simply bring pain to a small child who has no weapons against you."

"And if you want to know real satisfaction, stoop to help someone in need." Marlon's chest swelled, his grin sitting comfortably between his jowls. "How many times did I protect or defend you on that school yard?"

"Um, just the one time that I can think of, Bud. Maybe because you mention it so often -- "

"It wasn't about you anyway," Marlon said, waving him off. "It was about honor, it was about chivalry."

"It was about lunch money!" Wally's level, nasal tone brought Marlon back to the hallways of Lincoln Elementary. Marlon swaggered into his memory, once more the hulking, cocksure man-child of his youth. He could almost hear the slamming of the locker doors echoing down the hallway. For the ease of Marlon's imagination, Wally was no longer Wally at all, but the tough little bastard that always bullied him. Marlon could see the upturned nose and nasty grin, freckles and the red hair that made it look not only like his head was on fire but that he was enjoying it.

"Leave the little guy alone," Marlon said to Wally as the bully.

Wally turned in the perfect image of his own tormentor, even affecting that broad Illinois drawl. "*D'is* ain't no business o' y*rrrrrr*'s, big s*hah*t. Get l*aahhhs*st."

"It *is* my business." Marlon stepped forward.

Wally raised his hands to halt the advance of the imagined goons behind him. Glancing back at them, Wally said, "S'okay, boys, steady."

Marlon said, "When I see four cheap punks like you pickin' on one little guy, taking the few pennies he has left in the world, that makes it my business."

Wally stepped to the side with a curt, "Get him!" and Marlon leapt into the battle. One of many fights in his youth, Marlon brawled his way through the remembered crowd of eager toughs. His fists split skin and bone and time and space. The henchmen of his boyhood heroism fell back with spectacular followthrough, limbs splayed as his punches hurled their bodies backward.

The imagined face of Marlon's enemy stared back at him, portrayed by the very same person he was defending. Wally's bully ducked the first punch but could not avoid the second, an uppercut that sent the redheaded tormentor reeling back. Like a mask falling off Wally's head, his true face was revealed; a ready and grateful pup whose very life had just been spared.

"Thank you so much," Wally said, his natural voice slipping out of his thin lips. "I don't know what I would have done if you hadn't come along."

With a macho squint, Marlon said, "All in a day's work, *amigo*."

"I know you like to remember it that way." Wally stepped out of context if not out of character. "And it's true that fiction is much stranger and in this case a lot more heroic than fact, or else we'd both have been dentists or something."

"How do *you* remember it then?"

With a casual step forward in the study, Wally took Marlon back once more to that same hallway, that same day. Wally handed Marlon his glasses and assumed a familiar, almost simian posture.

He's doing me, Marlon realized, putting on the glasses to become Wally.

Around them, imagined children walked up and down the hall, books in hand, gossip passing in a murmured hum. Wally's Marlon pointed out one innocent passerby, a young man with red hair and freckles. He was minding his own business, even trying *not* to look at the menacing Marlon Brando Jr.

But in a pretty good vocal impression, Wally said to the imagined young man, "Hey, what're you looking at?" Wally turned to Marlon, who almost felt like he was having an out-of-body experience. "You see that look he gave you? Probably wants your lunch money. Guy in Kentucky gave me a look like that once. Now he still gives other people that same look, but he's just got the one good eye to do it with."

All Marlon could do was follow the rules of improvisation; never say no, stay in character. In Wally's nasal lisp, Marlon said, "Oh me, oh my," as he imagined Wally might have.

"You gonna sit there and take that? Be a man, stand up for yourself!"

"Uh, I *am* standing."

But Wally, as the young Marlon, was already approaching the red-haired kid, who in this version of the story looked around with considerable confusion and innocence. "Yeah, that's right," Wally's Marlon chided. "You wanna go a few rounds with Wally the Widow Maker then you have at it, tough guy."

Marlon fidgeted in the constraints of Wally's timidity. But if he couldn't fight, as Wally wouldn't have, he would talk the way Wally would have talked. "Uh, I really don't think this is a good idea. My solar plexus is currently in a state of *turbuncular* malfeasance. Additionally, I think I have an adenoidal disfunction in the -- "

"You think too much, bookworm. That's your problem."

"Well, I really can't imagine getting my head cracked open is the appropriate solution, much as it may appear otherwise." Marlon was getting comfortable in Wally's owlish persona, but Wally was clearly relishing his role as the brawlin' Marlon.

"What'd you say?" Wally's Marlon asked the redheaded kid, then he waited for an answer only he could hear. "Oh, just 'cause one guy helps out another *guy*, that means there's something goin' on? I'll show you what's goin' on!"

Wally's Marlon took the first swing. Even though it wasn't a miss, it was hardly decisive. The brawl played out with Wally's Marlon holding off a growing crowd of combatants. He took as much as he gave, and ultimately he stepped out of the contest weary on his feet like Terry Malloy at the climax of *On The Waterfront*. Wally dropped into the chair.

Marlon's Wally said, "Nobody could take a fall like you, Bud."

"I do like your version better." Not only was Wally resuming his own voice and mannerisms, allowing Marlon to do the same; he was once more the present-day, middle-aged Wally, back in Marlon's Hollywood Hills study.

Marlon said, "But as usual your memory is more accurate. You were always smarter than me, quicker."

"Smarter? Bud, you were a genius. You still are. I was merely brilliant. Even as a kid you were every bit as quick and talkative as I was. Of course, that was before all the mumbling." Slipping into his expert Marlon Brando impression, Wally continued, "The whole *Mr. Obtuse* thing."

Wally resumed his own voice, going from Marlon's visage to his own in the blink of an eye. "I was only keeping up. In other ways, I couldn't even do that."

"When did I ever make our friendship a competition?"

"Not when, *why*. But it takes two to have an argument, right? I guess I might have been a little jealous of your, uh, success with the ladies. I mean, who wouldn't want that kind of attention?"

The parade of women flashed before Marlon's memory, the deep well of resentment and conflict they inspired returning to his belly. Not a single relationship with any of his women had been worth a damn. *Doesn't Wally know this about me?* Marlon wondered. *What kind of friendship did we have?*

"Wally, all that with the girls, that wasn't me. That was my old man. He had girls too, drunken whores who weren't my mother."

The abrupt change of tone, from conciliatory to contentious, took Marlon by surprise. He lowered his voice to nearly a plead when he added, "That's not what I wanted out of life. Some people say I inherited his sexuality. I say I was cursed with it."

"He was always nice to me."

Quick images from his memory pulsed across Marlon's imagination; his father drunk on Christmas Eve and then happy on Christmas morning, the old man returning from a sales trip and the tantrum he would throw just a few hours later. The cold silence after the snap of his temper would hover over the kitchen table like the smell of bad fish.

"He was all right when he was sober. But when my father was drunk he was a brutal, ugly, hateful man; abusive to his friends, mean spirited. He was raised by his maiden aunts and they dressed him up like Little Lord Fauntleroy, with the blue velvet shorts and vest and the white knee socks. No wonder he turned into such a hard ass. You know that milking story in *Tango,* that really happened." Marlon had told him the story maybe a hundred times. In *Last Tango In Paris* he told the entire world. But he felt like telling it again, so Wally followed Marlon across the study. "I'm in my best clothes, real gone threads, man, on my way out the door. And he says -- "

"Where the hell do you think you're going?" Wally stood in front of Marlon; eyeglasses off, hands on his hips, brows stern over his eyes just like the old man's. His voice was even like Marlon Sr.'s.

Marlon said, "Basketball game, Pop."

Marlon walked past Wally and almost made it to the door before Wally's Marlon Sr. said, "Milk the cow?"

"I'll do it when I get home, Pop."

"Over my dead body." Marlon stopped and turned to face his father once more. "No son of mine's gonna shirk his chores to go prancing around at some ball game. Now turn your ass around and go take care of that cow before it gets dark."

Marlon stood in disbelief, almost smiling from the impossibility of the situation. "You can't be serious, Pop. I saved for months to buy these clothes. It's the big game. I'm not going out to milk any fucking cow."

Wally slapped him in the face, the crack of palm and cheek reverberating in Marlon's imagination. He could almost feel the sting, blood quivering under the skin. Wally's Marlon Sr. pointed his index finger into Marlon's face. "Don't you ever raise your voice to me or use that language in this house again! That cow helps pay for the roof over your head, which I own. Now get out there and do as you're told!"

Marlon turned, but not to the back door. "I'll change then."

"I said *now*, before it gets dark. You stupid lummox, you're more animal than man; maybe that cow should milk *you*!"

Even there in that cluttered Los Angeles home, years later, Marlon slumped in his defeat and shuffled toward where the cow would be. And from the past, Marlon Sr. offered a final insult.

"I swear I'll die with one regret; ever giving you my full name."

The old man disappeared back into memory. Wally stood with brows high, mouth closed, head turned with a ready ear. Marlon was glad to be back but still couldn't get the episode with his father out of his mind. "I went to the game with cow shit all over my shoes, my pants." The smell of dung and cigarettes and stale perfume raced back into Marlon's nostrils, challenging his brain to separate memory from reality.

"That was my old man in a nutshell," Marlon went on, "sent me out reeking of his miserable, shitty existence. It's amazing I accomplished anything at all. I tell ya, Wally, that'll never be me. I want to be the father that my father wasn't."

Without looking at Marlon, Wally said, "We all become our parents." After absorbing Marlon's contemptuous glare, Wally added, "Isn't that what they say?"

Another startling truth. But a ready distraction wasn't far off.

"How about a song, Wally?"

Chapter Three

The ukulele was red and small and light in Marlon's hands. He felt like a giant holding it.

Wally shook his head. "I think we should talk a little more about --"

"C'mon, it'll be fun," Marlon said. "It's been ages. And who knows when we'll have another chance like this?"

"There are more important things to discuss."

Marlon was already plucking out a *C* chord. "Let's do this one, from back in Evanston; one of the songs my mother taught me."

"Bud -- "

But the top of the verse arrived on the ukulele and Marlon sang the opening line to one of their favorite songs, Irving Berlin's *Mr. Jazz Himself.*

"I know a certain young fellow," Marlon sang, pausing to gauge Wally's reaction. "Who's filling the people with joy."

"I really don't think -- "

"How would you like to say hello," Marlon sang, the song moving steadily forward, "to this remarkable boy?"

"I *do* like Irving Berlin," Wally said.

Marlon sang, "People are talking about him, he's been the topic for days. He's a winsome gent with an instrument that pla*aaaayyyyyy*s ..."

In a flurry of quicker eighth notes, Marlon sang, "I'd like you all to meet him," before settling into the chorus melody. "Shake ha*aaaa*nds with Mr. Jazz himself, he took the saxophone from off the shelf ..."

Marlon thought he saw Wally moving to the rhythm. "And when you hear him play," Marlon sang, "you'll say he's been taking lessons up in he*eeeee*a-v*eee*en ..."

Now Wally joined in, their voices finding an easy, imperfect harmony. "That dreamy moan is his own 'riginality. He knows a certain kind of change in a minor key ... "

And before Marlon could sing it, Wally hit the eighth note run. "I don't know how he does it but -- "

"Wh*eeeee*n he starts to sing the blues," they sang together, "he's a messenger of happy news. No one could ever do it a*aaaaaa*s my friend Mr. J*aaaaaazz*."

Marlon's laughter was the tune's only applause, but it was appreciative and sincere. "Hey, remember back in New York, when we started hanging out again? Unbelievable how that came together. It had been over ten years since Evanston. And you stroll up, without missing a beat you say -- "

"Hi, Bud," Wally said, just as he had in New York in the nineteen-fifties.

"Hi, Wally. I'm having a little trouble getting Franny to take a ride with me in this shopping cart."

"Then there's a seat available? Let's do it!" Wally jumped onto the table as if it were the shopping cart Marlon hijacked back in New York. Marlon stood behind him, holding the rim of the tabletop as the cart's handles. He pushed off with one foot.

"Of course I had no idea you were going to send us careening out of control down Sixth Avenue."

Marlon smiled. "Grab their attention."

He certainly had grabbed Wally's. This memory triggered more enthusiasm and exuberance from him than Marlon had seen that night. Wally pointed ahead of them, voice high and loud. "Watch out for that truck pulling out!"

Marlon's imagination was alive with the sights and sounds of Manhattan's busy Sixth Avenue; pedestrians and cars, horses drawing handsome cabs and carrying policemen. Marlon could picture a fruit truck pulling out and spilling a load of watermelons into the street in front of them.

"Baby carriage!" Wally shouted.

Marlon leaned the table to his left to steer clear of the imagined obstacle. He swore he heard a woman's voice cry out, "My baby!"

Wally shrieked, "Open man hole, old man with a walker!" Each time Marlon pulled and leaned, teeth gritted in hopes of sparing the old man's life or their own from a grizzly end at the bottom of a sewer pipe.

"Cement mixer," Wally went on, "funeral procession!"

Marlon's back started to hurt. So as soon as his logical mind could escape the clutches of his eight-year-old's imagination, Sixth Avenue disappeared. Not that Marlon wasn't amused enough in his Los Angeles study watching Wally perched on his table, pretending to spearhead a runaway shopping cart.

"Marching band!" Wally cried out, gripping the table and leaning to steer. "Two guys carrying a pane of glass!" Marlon couldn't help but chuckle.

"President of the United States! Bank robbery in progress! Electrified f*eeeeennnnnnn*ce ..." Wally shook the table beneath him, vibrating and giving his punch line a jittering, electrocuted sound effect. He seemed genuinely stunned and took a moment to sigh and look around.

"No guy on a stretcher?" Marlon asked.

"He was dead by the time the paramedics arrived."

As Wally crawled off the table, Marlon took a few steps toward a bowl of pistachios and a smaller bowl for the shells. "I always said you had the mentality of a serial killer, Wally."

"Cops thought so too. Remember how they used to drag me in for every rape, kidnapping, flashing?"

"Maybe if you hadn't rode your motorcycle up the steps of Town Hall, you'd have made a better impression." Even the slightest recollection of little Wally pushing his big Harley up those marble steps brought a smile to Marlon's face.

"It didn't make me a child molester."

Marlon shrugged, peeling a pistachio from its shell and popping it into his mouth. "You fit the type. Luckily you got famous, or else you'd have spent the rest of your adult life in and out of night court."

"All the less time I'd have to spend with that filthy beast you kept around the apartment."

"Maureen Stapleton?" Reading Wally's impatient expression, Marlon winked. "Russell was a good pet and a good friend."

"Russell was a raccoon, Bud. And you knew me, I loved animals. But this creature of yours, I was always afraid I was going to wake up in the middle of the night to find it nibbling on one of my ears. And it soiled the entire place."

Marlon smiled. "Are you sure you're not talking about one of your girlfriends, Wally?"

"No, Bud. I said nibbling on *my* ears, not *yours*."

That hurt; a blade forged from Marlon's own indiscretions, thrusting into his conscience. But it was hardly fatal.

"So what's it like, Wally?" Marlon looked up at the ceiling and past it, Wally doing the same. "Y'know, up there."

"How do *you* think it would be?"

"The best of everything, Wally, I'm sure. Just like you deserve." Marlon stepped closer to Wally with straightened posture, an ingratiating smile and a bad English butler's accent resembling David Niven's.

"Good evening, Mr. Cox, welcome to heaven. All of your needs and tastes have been catered to. There's plenty of snow on the mountain, your sled is dry and ready. Nobody here over four feet tall, so we've no worries in that regard. Bourbon flows out of the tap, you'll appreciate *that* I'm sure."

"And what about *you*, Bud? Don't you deserve the best?" Marlon waved him off, but Wally wouldn't be distracted again. "*Candy*, Bud? *The Nightcomers*? Why didn't you ask more for yourself and *from* yourself?"

Marlon could only review the sad parade of failures. "When I was a kid, you know how it was. I did pretty well with *Streetcar*."

"You were a phenomenon, Bud, I don't think anyone could doubt that. After you, the entire craft of acting was changed forever."

Marlon's eyes lit up with images from his youth, each caught in a camera's flash; the tuxedos and the premieres, the parties and the women and the men. Then they trailed off, leaving just the occasional burst of a photographer's bulb to capture the growing bulk, the graying hair.

"But that first blush of fame doesn't last," Marlon said. "If you look at my unsuccessful films, from the sixties most of them, what you see is my attempt to turn that early phenomenon into something real, something lasting. I was making art, but they're all in the shit business."

"That's the new America for you," Wally said, raising the snifter and swirling the cognac in his palm. "'We agree with what you say, but will defend not at all your right to say it.'"

"Exactly. Same thing happened to Orson Welles after *Ambersons*."

Marlon read the look creeping over Wally's features; head titled forward, eyebrows raised in disbelief, glasses sliding down the nose. The look said, *You're comparing yourself to the great Orson Welles?*

Marlon stood up and stretched, pacing to reason it out. "Well, why not? We both peaked early, both beaten down by the studio system, had our best work butchered by neophytes. Both got fat."

"You're not that fat, Bud. Yet."

"I'll always be fat." By then the ukulele was already in Marlon's hands, and the tune that popped into his head proved irresistible. "Brando," he sang to the jaunty melody of *Meet the Flintstones*. "Marlon Brando, he's the fattest guy in histor*yyyyyyyyy*y. There's his buddy Wally, he's the cutest guy you'll ever se*eeeeeee*e."

Wally laughed and Marlon couldn't help but chuckle too. Then that bubbling giddiness faded in Marlon's mind and heart to make room for rank bitterness and drunken aggression. He pointed at Wally with the ukulele like it was a red, wooden finger. "But I'll never get screwed again, I'll tell you that. No matter what happens, Brando gets his from now on! You should see some of the deals I have lined up."

"I'm happy for you, Bud. I wish *you* were a little happier." After a tense pause, Wally added, "Acting used to make you happy, didn't it?"

Marlon didn't have to think about it for long. "When I was acting, especially early on, I felt I could be as far from my father's influence as possible. I could be loose and free, repulsive and undisciplined."

"When you were acting? Bud, you can't sit still. You can't keep your mind on one project for an adequate stretch. There are times when you can't even finish a thought before going on to something else."

"Exactly, that's acting in a nutshell."

"What, disarray?" Wally raised his hands to the disheveled mess around them. "A chaotic nightmare, a good thing gone rotten?"

"Yes! In the end acting is just a bunch of bullshit, ladled out by producers to distributors and on to consumers. It may be loose, but it ain't free. Maybe I should have stayed on stage in New York instead of coming out to Hollywood, I dunno. So many conflicting points of view on a single project, all kinds of variables, expenses. Jobs are on the line. It ain't ever easy, Wally, you know that. If the picture's a hit, all the grief will be forgotten. But when the picture is bad, all you can do is stick a lampshade on your head and stand real still, hope that nobody notices you."

And Marlon knew that as many of his failures were noble and well intentioned as were simply paychecks stapled to bad reviews. He'd fail all over again to make another *Burn!* or *The Ugly American*. He was risking it all to do *Wounded Knee,* a film that could reverse years of discrimination and hostility.

"Your recent films were big hits though," Wally said, "commercially and artistically. *Godfather, Tango*; you didn't do those for the money."

"I did 'em *both* for the money! They happened to be great films, for reasons other than me. I was lucky to get 'em and I worked damn hard. Stephanie Beecham and I went over all my films, this was during the *Nightcomers* shoot. And it turns out that all the good ones, *Burn!* and *Waterfront* and *Jacks*, they were painful, difficult experiences. *Tango* was a real bear, Wally."

Memories of that long and difficult Paris shoot, the constant emotional tumult the characters and thus the actors had to endure, came back to Marlon as if he'd just walked off the set. He closed his eyes to blot it out, pinching the base of his nose and this time in genuine pain.

"If that's acting," Marlon went on, "and I think it has to be, then I'm through. It's just too painful. And I'm not the only one; making *Streetcar* nearly drove Vivien Leigh insane."

"Not a very long drive, from what I understand," Wally said. "Is that why you use the cue cards?"

"Oh hell no, didn't we ever talk about this? I used cards on all my best pictures. Look, in real life a person doesn't know what they're gonna say from one moment to the next. You'll never sound realistic if you're just waiting to repeat some memorized bullshit. If I can read it for the first time just before saying it, just like I was thinking it right then and there, without any time to add any fakery or representation, that's what gives it that reality."

Dodie's face was clear in Marlon's memory, finger pointing at him with sternness and support. "Don't act," Marlon said to Wally just as Dodie had said to him. "Let the lines speak for themselves."

Wally listened with a quizzical expression as Marlon turned his ear to an imagined tune. "She used to love *Rites Of Spring*. Familiar with it?"

"By Stravinsky, yes."

"Played it all the time." Marlon dropped his sluggish weight into the chair. "God I hated that music."

After a long, still silence, Wally said, "Bud?"

"Y'know my grandparents, Dodie's folks, were truly spiritual people. They were never impressed with the conventional definitions of success; materialism, greed." Marlon could still conjure their blurred faces, yellowing like old photos. "They always encouraged me to find a way outside the norm, beyond the boundaries of civilization."

"Maybe that explains your fixation with Tahiti."

"Perhaps you're right, Dr. Cox," Marlon said, a smile curling under his nose. "Imagine, a Freudian named Cox. But that doesn't help me with the screw sticking in my abdomen."

Wally saw the gag and raised his imagined note pad. "Why don't you have the screw removed?"

"I did. My ass fell off."

This surreal image always delighted Marlon for some reason he couldn't explain, even if it left most people scratching their heads. As usual, Wally didn't miss a beat.

"Your ass? That must have left quite a crater."

Marlon said, "Yes, it -- hey, I thought you said I wasn't that fat."

"I said *yet*. We were talking about acting?"

"Were we talking *about* it or talking *at* it?"

"I think we were reading it from cue cards."

The cue cards, Marlon thought. *Forget the Indians and Tahitians, the civil rights efforts, the awards. Years after I'm gone, all they'll be talking about is fat-ass Marlon Brando and his fucking cue cards.*

Marlon said, "They don't make acting any easier, y'know. You gotta figure out how to get from one card over here to one on the other side of the room, work it all into the scene without distracting the director. Also you have to keep in mind what kind of lens the camera is using, where the light is coming from. It doesn't matter what happens on the set, Wally, but what the camera *sees* happening on the set."

Wally nodded like he understood, but Marlon had his doubts. Nobody seemed to understand.

Marlon said, "Movies are shit now anyway."

"You think so? Seems to me future generations'll look back on this as one of cinema's golden ages."

"Proves my point; the American people have lost their way."

"You're right about that, Bud. Celebrity is a fine diversion, movies and all. But some people become enamored of it on both sides of the screen. Television has made it too easy for people to become abnormally attached to their favorite stars. It's frightening."

"It's those gossip rags," Marlon said. "*National Enquirer*, all that."

"'Enquiring minds want to know.'"

"They wanna know too damn much! And it'll only get worse." Marlon liberated a pistachio from its red shell and inhaled the tender nugget of meat. "You should hear what Bob Dylan had to deal with. They were going through his garbage, man, climbing up on his roof in the middle of the night. After the whole Manson Family thing, it's no joke."

"All the more reason to keep Christian from prowling around the neighbors' houses." Marlon glared at Wally, but Marlon knew the real subject of his own contempt; he was taller and fatter and a lot more famous. Not even the great Marlon Brando could save young Christian.

"You know how it is when you're divorced, Wally. You've only got so much time, how can you really influence them?"

Even as Marlon said it he knew how feeble it sounded, how weak and contemptible. No brief lapses in time could interrupt truly good parenting. Their separation was simply a challenge, one to be met and overcome.

So Marlon added, "What am I supposed to say? *Don't experiment, don't make mistakes.* After my life? He wouldn't buy it and neither would I."

"You could teach him that breaking and entering is a crime, how about starting with that?"

"I've yelled, I've reasoned, I've bargained and bribed." Marlon's memory was fresh with the scattered scenes of his struggles with Christian's indestructible will to self-destruct. "I've tried psychology, psychiatry, obscenity, blasphemy, tolerance, *in*tolerance."

Wally didn't answer. There was no time and no need.

"I've sat him down, right here." Marlon leaned forward, closer to Wally. Marlon's view blurred from hallucination to memory until he wasn't seeing Wally at all but young Christian himself, staring up with those big, dark eyes.

"Baby, you're killing yourself with these people, these drugs, all the boozing." In Marlon's mind's eye, Christian sat with a slouch, forever gloomy and unimpressed. "I love you so much, Son, and my heart breaks when I think of what could happen if you don't start making better choices."

"Why don't you teach him by example?" Wally asked, replacing Christian. "That's why he's in this mess in the first place, because he learned from watching you. I love you so much, Bud, and *my* heart breaks when I think of what could happen if you don't start making better choices."

"Talk about bad choices, I never wanted to be a dramatic actor at all. I always thought comedy would be more my thing. Forget Monty Clift or James Dean, I really wanted to be Oliver Hardy. Can you imagine that in *Tango*?"

Marlon's interior vision suddenly used a sepia-toned filter, their world flickering and scratched like an old print of some classic film comedy. Fidgeting with a necktie that wasn't there, Marlon rolled his eyes in his best impression of the obese comic Hardy. "Wally, I want you to get the fucking butter and then stick your fingers up my ass."

Wally started to whimper in a perfect impression of Stan Laurel; brows arching upwards, hand pulling at his hair, his voice a whining stream of rolling vowels.

Marlon's Oliver asked, "What's the matter, Wally?"

Words barely comprehensible in his baying, Wally's Stan Laurel said, "I don't want to stick my fingers up your ass, Bud!" A muted trumpet in the back of Marlon's ear brought them out of the scene and into his study. But he wasn't there for three seconds before Wally turned the whole place into a television studio, complete with live audience. Wally looked into the imaginary camera as it rolled slowly toward him.

"Hello, welcome back to *The Wally Cox Program*. With us tonight is a very special guest, a hero of American Indian culture -- "

"No, Wally."

"One of the greatest figures of the Old West," Wally said into the camera.

"How am I supposed to play it so I don't sound like fucking Tonto?"

"What does fucking Tonto sound like? 'Oh, Tonto, yes, that's so good! Unmask me, Tonto!'" Marlon wasn't amused. Displaying as much calmness as Marlon was growing hostility, Wally said, "Why don't you just trot out that hammy Irish accent you're always falling back on?"

"Hammy?" Marlon had to repeat it to make sure he'd heard his old friend correctly. "Y'know, there are over thirty distinct Irish accents."

"And you do them all ... at once."

Not only couldn't he believe Wally would say such things but, as he asked himself in amazement, *In front of a live studio audience?* Marlon looked at them, seated in escalating rows of imaginary seats behind the imaginary cameras in the imaginary studio. "Are we live?" he asked Wally, a reminder more than a question. "You better finish your introduction."

"Sitting Bull, ladies and gentlemen!" The audience's applause rose and fell and Wally turned back to Marlon. "Shall I call you Sitting Bull or Mr. Bull?"

Marlon cleared his throat. He jutted his chin and pulled his tongue back. In a halting, steady tone, emitted from the chest, Marlon said, "First name Sitting, last name Bull. Perhaps you have heard of some other members of Bull family. There my cousin, Slinging Bull; my brother, Unemploya Bull; him hot wife, Totally Fucka -- "

"Now Now, Mr. Bull," Wally said, chuckling nervously. "This is a family program." Wally scanned the table, picking up an invisible box about the size of his palm. He held it up and faced the camera. "*Lifebouy* brand soap bar; uh, cleans your mouth inside *and* out!"

Wally set down the box and turned back to Marlon's Sitting Bull. "I understand that Hollywood is trying to make a motion picture about your life, to star the famous actor Marlon Brando. What do you think of that, Chief?"

"This Brando," Marlon's Sitting Bull said, "him have forked tongue. Sitting Bull not mean Brando not speak truth, only that him eat so much, tongue has turned into fork. Him spear food and pull it in, leave hands free to grab more. You white men must consider him a god."

"Some do."

"Him greatly feared by enemies."

Wally asked, "You mean injustice, bigotry and war?"

"No; steak, chop and baked potato." A quick pang of hunger turned in Marlon's belly, and rubbing it brought no satisfaction. Dropping the character like a boring toy, Marlon said, "I'm gettin' hungry."

Wally looked at Marlon in a long, considered silence. "Do you really feel that big?"

"Did you really feel that small?" *Aha,* Marlon thought, *now I gotcha. After running amok with my conscience, I've got* you *on the ropes.*

"I guess I may have had my own ways of overcompensating," Wally said, looking down with slight embarrassment.

"Wally, you built a house all by yourself, from the ground up; electricity, plumbing, everything."

"Well, not *entirely* by myself."

Marlon had to stand, pacing to give himself the feel, the movement of a life like Wally's. "From a weak little boy to a one-man construction crew. And the weightlifting, the upper body work; no wonder you wear that baggy suit. Underneath it you look like Popeye the Sailor! And all the macho, outdoorsy stuff? You had something to prove. It's okay, we all do."

"It wasn't for show, Bud. The rock climbing and the hiking, those were the only times I didn't have to think about all that other stuff. On a mountain, nobody's *that* tall."

"Wally, I didn't mean -- "

"You think I needed to be seen toughing it up with the great Marlon Brando just to prove I wasn't really Robinson *Mr. Goodboy* Peepers?"

Marlon had rarely seen Wally this upset; the spittle jumping off his slight lisp, hair dangling down over his broad, round forehead. Wally said, "It's weird, isn't it? As an actor you want to be successful -- "

"I thought you didn't care about being famous."

"Not as much as *some* people. But I didn't become an actor in hopes of one day being obscure! Then you get stuck in a certain character and nobody cares to accept you as anything else. People have this perception and you come to resent it. The very thing that made you famous, that gave you what you wanted all along, becomes the thing you hate the most."

"You're in good company," Marlon said, reaching for the snifter but finding it in Wally's hand. "Robert Zimmerman *hates* Bob Dylan. Talk about a mumbler! Zimmy keeps trying to kill him, but the little mush-mouthed bastard won't die! Colonel David Crockett used the hillbilly Davy character to sell books and swindle voters."

"And Crockett paid the price."

"It was the colonel who paid at the Alamo. Davy Crockett lives on. So will Bob Dylan."

A swallow of cognac didn't bring Wally any solace. "Robinson Peepers is no Davy Crockett."

"Different as *you* and Peepers were," Marlon said, "there were similarities. He was a moralist, just like you, always sticking up for the little guy."

"Just like you."

"I guess you're right, we're like peas in a pod." Marlon grabbed the ukulele. Hitting a country two-step, he sang, "I am the eggman, he was the eggman ..."

And before he could finish the chorus, Wally chimed in with, "I am the Wallace."

They sang the famous refrain together. "*Koo-koo-ka-choo!*"

Marlon and Wally were left to flounder in their mutual memory of the swirling colors, flowery patterns, sitar sounds and trippy optimism of that defunct decade, the sixties. "Now I ask you," Wally said, "how could *Mr. Peepers* ever have competed in the world of psychedelic rock and LSD?"

"It *was* primitive television," Marlon said, lower lip creeping up to punctuate his summation. "And George Burns broke the fourth wall to much better effect on *his* show."

"Well gee, Bud, like I said it wasn't *that* bad a program. It was a big hit, in fact."

"And the casting? Tony Randall as a preening jackass? Who'd'a thunk it?"

"I *did* win the Motion Picture Daily Fame Award as Television's Most Promising Male Star."

"You sure did, Wally, and that's quite an honor. I think my Oscars are gang-raping it in the other room even as we speak."

"Oscars plural?"

"The one from *Waterfront* is imagining the one from *Godfather* is there with him, just like I'm imagining you're -- " But he couldn't finish. Such realization was dangerous, Marlon knew. It could drive Wally away, perhaps for good.

But Wally just smiled in his understanding of their reunion's delicacy. "It's okay, Bud. I'm glad to see you under any circumstances. And in truth I only wish I'd sent an Eskimo or something to refuse my Fame award, they'd still be talking about it today."

"They'll forget us all eventually. You remember the fifties? We were the revolution."

Images of the broad-chested Wild One staring handsomely from atop his roaring hog crackled in Marlon's memory. The brutal Stanley Kowalski, *Waterfront's* tortured Terry Malloy; *We?* Marlon asked himself and didn't have to wait long for the correction.

"Well, *you* were." The thick eyeglasses, the shuffling mannerisms; to the people, Wally *was* Eisenhower's America. He was born of industry, raised by science, all the animal squeezed out of him by his own precious civilization.

"As far as the world was concerned," Wally went on, "I was what they were rebelling against."

"Then the sixties left us both in the dust. What a washout *that* revolution was."

"Most of them are. That's why time keeps marching on, it'd be embarrassed to hang around the scenes of all its failures." *Here it comes,* Marlon said to himself. *Wally's riffing.*

Wally added, "Length, height and width just sit and do nothing. You can walk right up, measure them with a ruler, and they'll just wait patiently. But time, the one naughty dimension, makes *you* wait instead. If you do try to measure it, you have to wait until some of it marches on. And forget about using a ruler!"

Marlon tried to think of something to top it, something funnier or more clever. As it so often happened, Marlon came up empty. "I always thought you were one of the great comics, Wally; in the Chaplin line, and I mean that. Where would Bob Newhart or Woody Allen be without you?"

"They're both very talented men, Bud, I'm sure they'd be doing ..." Wally smiled, "... *almost* as well as they are now."

"Will Rogers, O. Henry, even Lenny Bruce."

Wally's head ducked with humility, then turned with consideration. "Why not? If *you* can be Orson Welles."

"And your monologues; the fat kid who couldn't get over the fence, the scout master who got his troop lost on the way back to camp, the guy who takes his dog to the psychiatrist -- "

"That one's gonna happen, mark my words. The way therapy is spreading across America, people'll be taking their ferns in for treatment. One day everyone'll be insane."

"Best way to achieve normalcy, just lower the standard." With a sudden sarcasm in his tone, Marlon added, "Thanks for mentioning me in your book, by the way."

"Oh, you read *My Life As A Young Boy*?" Wally's voice was buoyant again, as if trying to soothe Marlon's wounded ego.

"I read 'em both, that one and *Ralph Makes Good*."

"I also wrote a children's book, *The Tenth Life Of Osiris Oaks*."

But the sad fact of the books' piddling sales hung in the air, the stink of failure.

"I just can't believe you didn't have greater success, Wally. Why do you think that is? Didn't you want the best from life, for yourself and *from* yourself?"

Chapter Four

Wally smiled, gazing into his memory. "Once I was on my way to the set of *Hollywood Squares* and I came upon this butterfly, a beautiful Lorquin's Admiral. You should have seen it, Bud. I followed that little guy halfway to Nevada, just to see where it was going and to watch it get there. I'm amazed I didn't crash, I barely took my eyes off it for over an hour."

"I'm still amazed you were doing *Hollywood Squares*."

Wally tossed his hands up, shaking his head. "Everybody knocks *Squares*. But it's the funniest game show since Groucho's, gets terrific ratings. Saved my ass, I'll tell you that; Paul's too, and a lot of other people's."

"So did penicillin, but I wouldn't wanna sit around watching it on TV."

Wally tapped Marlon on the forearm, guiding him back to the point. "For me, the best things in life didn't come from being on a TV show or a film set, Bud. I may have been content to hawk my jewelry, but at least I didn't take it upon myself to save an entire art form, not to mention a near-extinct race of people."

"They need saving, Wally." The tragedies, the lost lives, the lies and broken promises; Marlon couldn't escape the mountain of horrors. "Governments so corrupt, men so stupid and inept."

"Stupidity, largely misidentified as corruption by the unthinking."

But before Marlon could take offense, Wally added, "And dirty government? That's nobody's idea of a good time. Without the dirty money and the dirty girls and the dirty laughs, what's the point?"

Marlon recognized their dance. They'd always done this, rebut and retort and contradict for the sheer joy of trying to outthink the other. How many parties had they entertained with this conversational counterpoint, Marlon couldn't fathom a guess. But he was getting an idea of how many parties they might have *spoiled* doing it.

"Look what we're doing to the planet, Wally."

"It's great that you care so much, Bud. But even in the event of all-out nuclear devastation, the planet itself would ultimately recover. It might take millions of years, and Lord knows what would grow here after us; but *something* would, that's for sure."

"And what about your own race?"

Wally could only sigh. "Have you noticed that the human race is the only race that criticizes the human race? Plus, it's the only race that shows any concern at all for the other races."

"Easy for you to say that, now that you're dead. You think the world'll just take care of itself, that I should stick my head up my ass like everybody else?"

"No, but like so many U. S. presidents, and other world leaders too, I think you're concerning yourself with foreign matters while your domestic front is crumbling."

Marlon rapped his palm against the tabletop and pointed at Wally. "Politics, exactly. What about Vietnam, Watergate? Don't you think those are signs that our civilization is on the brink?"

"As long as we learn from those mistakes. Can you imagine another secluded, elitist, corrupt White House administration like Nixon's, or the U. S. stumbling headlong into another untenable situation like Vietnam?"

There had to be another way to get through to Wally. Marlon picked up the phone. "Hello, Department of Denial? I have someone here you should talk to; he could run your entire western division."

But Wally'd played this little game before. He picked up an imaginary phone that just happened to be sitting right in front of him. "No, sir, I'm afraid you've reached the Office of the Obvious and Oblivious. We've got a serious situation here with a man who's trying to solve the world's problems because he can't face the troubles in his own life. Could you hold?"

Marlon grabbed his crotch and said, "Hold *this*," before hanging up the phone.

"I certainly applaud your willingness to take on the bigger

opponent." Wally leapt to his feet and clapped his hands once. Then he pointed out an invisible spectator in a crowd of imagined onlookers. In the looping whine of a turn-of-the-century freak show talker, commonly miscalled a barker, Wally said, "Step right up, ladies and gentlemen, step right up. Come one, come all for a glimpse of the Amazing Marlon; able to take on the mightiest giants and bring the dead back to life. He led a generation of actors out of bondage, folks! He's defied the will of kings and, even more impressively, movie producers. The Amazing Marlon, ladies and gents; he's King David, Jesus, Moses and Elijah all rolled into one!"

"'Aim high,' that's my motto."

Back in his own timid demeanor, Wally said, "Mine was always, 'Walk softly and carry a little twig.'"

"'And hurt a minimum of people.' That's a dangerously old-fashioned outlook."

Wally said, "I was modern enough in my way."

"You were certainly a pioneer of modern therapy. I don't know anybody who kept at it as long as you did; especially considering the effects, or lack thereof."

"Sure, I was in therapy." Wally took a few casual steps around the study. "I didn't want to be the last one. But I found out that I wasn't nearly as crazy as I thought. I had a chemical imbalance."

"Wally, you grew up under unusual circumstances, with your mother an' all, then struggling with your own sexual identity -- "

"No, Bud; that was *your* problem, not mine."

"That's where you're wrong, Wally." Marlon stood and turned to face him. "Like a lot of men, I've had homosexual experiences. I don't deny that."

"The fits of rage, the mood swings, the manipulative withdrawals, the aggressive womanizing; classic homosexual anxiety."

"So it took some time for me to get used to. I was in therapy too, Wally." Marlon reached for the pistachios, musing at the irony of picking this moment to pop some nuts into his mouth. "I was never more secretive about my bisexuality than society demanded, even less with family and friends. My life's an open book."

"Written in invisible ink. And mine seemed to be in a foreign language. So my doctor put me on these pills -- "

"Too many pills in America, Wally. The Indians know that. Those aren't remedies, they're new diseases. Canada has it right with that government-run health care, that's what we need." Marlon sat, gobbling another pistachio and talking as he chewed. "Too many private interests to be served otherwise, too much money to be made. The welfare of the patient is bound to suffer."

"They got their share of *my* money, that's for sure."

"Did the pills work?"

After a moment to consider, Wally said, "I wasn't on them long, unfortunately. At first they helped, then they seemed to make my mood swings more severe. The doctors felt I would stabilize after not too long."

"You stabilized all right." Marlon drew a horizontal line in front of himself and made a spit-filled fart sound, tongue sticking out; a reference to Wally's permanent state of rest. After a brief chuckle, Marlon said, "I'm sorry, Wally, I know that was in bad taste."

But Wally chuckled too. "S'okay, Bud. Who gets a chance to laugh at his own death? Kind of makes laughing at your life all the easier."

The room got heavy and still, Marlon's palms clammy. He reached out, pinching Wally on the cheek. Wally blocked with a windmill defense, but Marlon's other hand was ready to tweak his unprotected nipple.

"Cut it out, Bud!"

But that was really an invitation for more, despite Wally's impatient, "Knock it off!" A fourth pinch, under Wally's left armpit, inspired Wally to grab Marlon's right hand, elbows clacking against the tabletop.

"Arm wrestle, right now," Wally said, grabbing Marlon's other free hand with his. Their fingers clung between them, fists quivering with the pressure. Marlon gritted his teeth, muscles stretching across his arm and shoulder. Wally's face was getting redder and Marlon was glad to see it.

"I know you inside and out, Wally. You're like an organ; I know just what pedals to push, what keys to play."

A little smile wriggled under Wally's graying mustache. "That's your mistake, Bud. I'm more like a saxophone, so you're gonna have to blow me!" With a burst of strength, Wally pushed Marlon's fist backward and onto the table. They released their grip and pulled back, rubbing their forearms.

"So how come you never got me on *Squares* anyway? I would'a been great on that show."

Wally said, "I can imagine," and so could Marlon. He saw himself sitting in that brightly lit sound stage, behind the little desk in one of the stacked cubicles. Wally, as genial host Peter Marshall, pretended to look at a small card in his hand and then up at Marlon.

Wally's Peter said, "Marlon, Europeans call it *wooden mouth*. What do *you* call it?"

"I don't know," Marlon answered, "but it's twenty dollars extra." After the studio audience's laughter faded into the recesses of Marlon's brain, a few scraps of imagery remained to tantalize. "Hey, Wally, what's the deal with Paul Lynde and that pretty girl, Karen something -- ?"

"Valentine."

"There's something goin' on there, right? C'mon, you can tell me."

Wally tilted his head to imagine what Marlon was inferring; a sexual union between the swishy, bronzed Paul Lynde, shrill in his medallions and silk shirts and the perky, wholesome Karen Valentine, brown hair cascading over her freshly scrubbed features.

"Uh gee, Bud, they're very close, I know that much. Y'know, we used to go to dinner together every Thursday night between tapings. She tells him all about her boyfriends, he does the same. He's her best friend, like a girlfriend. But you know about Paul, he and Karen couldn't ever be -- "

"Don't you see, Wally? That's the tragedy of their doomed love. She's America's sweetheart and he's the reigning queen of TV; best friends, coworkers. But he's secretly in love with her, a reaction that astounds him. Even though it seems to contradict every fiber of his being, still her name hangs in his heart like a golden bell , and when he hears it the bell swings and rings *Karen Valentine, Karen Valentine* -- "

"Uh, Bud, you're doing *Cyrano de Bergerac* again."

"Right!" Marlon clapped once to punctuate Wally's insight and to pat him symbolically on the back, the ancient origin of applause. "It's a modern-day, homosexual *Cyrano*. He knows he can never have her so he pines beneath his cavalier facade. All the while his soul withers and dies. Paul drinks?"

Wally thought about it for a moment, only then realizing that he was about to take a sip of cognac himself. He set the snifter down. "I can't say from any immediate experience for obvious reasons. But he's been known to."

"If he's nursing a broken heart with liquor, you'll have company sooner than you expect." Marlon tried not to think of himself, that cognac burning its way through his liver and kidneys. But there was no reason to dwell on his own challenges when Wally's were right there for the picking. And it was a bumper crop. "Y'know, you weren't supposed to drink while you were taking those pills, Wally. Maybe that's why your moods were so volatile."

Wally glared at him; brows low, mouth an angry, flat line. Even his voice was frowning. "How would you know? When I died, it'd been over a year since we'd really spoken."

A cold shock pulsed through Marlon's blood, curling in his guilty stomach. The hairs on his arms stood against him. "I'm sorry about that, Wally. I didn't know how little time there was left. I didn't know how bad off you were. Your depression was severe?"

Wally stood, arms flopping at his sides as he took his turn around the cluttered room. "You know how it is, Bud. Some days I couldn't get outta bed, other days I was terrified to go home. It's like laughing your head off and crying your eyes out at the same time."

Marlon did know. He'd been hanging by a thread for years. And he knew how close he was to hearing that thread snap, the way Wally did.

Marlon said, "Is it true then?" Wally looked away. "Is it true ... that you killed yourself, Wally?"

Wally leaned forward with a mischievous grin. "What planet is closest to the sun?"

Marlon repeated it to himself. *A trick question?* he wondered. *A hint about the suicide? A way to dodge the matter entirely?* Marlon answered, "Mercury."

"Furthest?"

"Are you patronizing me?" Marlon stood, posture erect. "Sir, I take that as an insult!" Marlon pulled an imagined glove from his nonexistent breast pocket and slapped it across Wally's face from a foot or so away. Well out of reach, Wally still took the slaps with his head snapping to one side and then the other. He looked back at Marlon and assumed an on guard stance, legs splayed with one hand holding an unseen foil and the other dangling behind for balance.

"On guard," Marlon said, taking the same position. He advanced with a cut to Wally's head and could almost hear the blades clink and scrape.

Wally said, "Mambo," with a parry *in seconde*.

"Samba," Marlon retorted, feinting left.

"Tango." Wally advanced with a perfect lunge and a cut to the chest. But Marlon's mind went blank as he searched for the response. Wally's trap was sprung and their swords locked.

Wally said, "Flamenco, you putz."

"Damn you, Scarlet *Wimp*ernell!" They pushed away from each other, swords slicing the stagnant air as Marlon drove Wally back.

Wally said, "Teapot Dome scandal."

Marlon deceived Wally's parry, remaining on the offensive. "Nineteen-twenty."

"Twenty-two." Marlon felt Wally's blade cut across the muscle of his thigh. But it was merely a flesh wound. Marlon continued his advance. "*Moby Dick*."

"Eighteen-fifty-one."

"Ah-ha!" Marlon dealt Wally a flurry of cuts to the head and chest, nearly pinning him to the wall. "Eighteen-fifty."

"Fifty-one, I'm afraid." Wally's parry *in quinte* halted Marlon's advance. "You can check it out, I think you have a copy around here somewhere. McKinnley assassinated?"

"Nineteen-oh-one."

In the style of a classic Bond villain, Wally said, "Very good, Mr. Bud."

Marlon delighted in Wally's choice. In what he always felt was a pretty good Sean Connery impression, all bubbling spit and meaty throat, Marlon answered, "Well then, Dr. Peepers, perhaps you can list all Seven Dwarves."

Wally stepped into his attack, a broad strike of the blades for every dwarf's name. "Doc." *Clack!* "Dopey." *Clang!* "Happy, Sleepy, Bashful, Grumpy ..." The names ran dry, Wally freezing before delivering the seventh strike.

Marlon relished the opening. "Now who's the putz?" His muttered chuckle had particular venom as he poised his own blade. But before he could deliver that fateful strike, Wally said, "Sneezy."

Marlon's blade was diverted in its lethal course, nearly sent flying out of his hand.

Wally said, "Victory is mine!" before lowering his sword and thrusting his chest like the hero of his childhood fantasies.

Now Marlon had to step into the role of villain. So he raised his sword on Wally and ran him through, piercing the heart. Wally turned to Marlon with wide eyes and a terrified quiver. He gasped, clutching the blade, voice creaking. "But why?"

Marlon pulled his sword from Wally's chest with a swishy sound effect. "To prove a point," Marlon said as Wally fell to the floor. "Nobody can take a fall like me."

But it was to Marlon's surprise that Wally was already on his feet and standing behind him. He pulled Marlon's head back, palm flat against his forehead, and drew an invisible knife blade across Marlon's throat.

"If you wonder what that sound is that's wakin' you, it's your own throat bein' cut." Wally stepped back to leave Marlon sagging in his death.

"Hey, that's pretty good," Marlon said. "Think I'll use it."

"Help yourself."

Marlon got the reference, Wally's plea; *help yourself.* They'd put down their swords, but the duel continued. And there were things Marlon wanted to know before the final thrust home. There were things he wanted to say. But they welled up inside him, jamming his mind and his conscience and his coward's quivering yellow belly.

"I miss you so much, Wally."

"I know, Bud. I miss you too. I miss all this stuff; the goofing around, wrestling, climbing rocks. I miss my friends, I miss making love to my wife. I miss *Underdog*."

"We all do, Wally." The little yellow dog in the red suit and floppy black ears came streaming back into Marlon's memory, along with the show's couplets and odd gangster villains. *Overcat?* Marlon remembered. *Hilarious*!

"But you did so much," Marlon said. "Seems to me you were working all the time. You were in *Barefoot Executive* when I couldn't get arrested in Hollywood. TV, books; what did you care anyway? You had your Harley and your butterflies."

Wally stared off, reflecting. "Yeah, my agent was more upset about my career than I was."

"Still, you did keep a rather dark outlook on life. And I don't blame you after what happened with that bitch."

"There's no need for that kind of language, Bud." Wally tried to shrug it off, but Marlon was already hulking toward him in a new and horrible guise.

"Wally, you come home and find your wife in bed with another man." Marlon picked Wally up by the lapels and pulled him to his feet. "Then the guy starts beating you, nearly to death?" And Marlon, as his friend's tormentor, began pulling broad, menacing punches to Wally's vigorous recoil.

"That deserves any kind of language you can think of and then some," Marlon said. "Call the longshoremen and have them send their brightest talent, they won't do it justice by half!"

"It did bring up uncomfortable memories of my mother. Fidelity didn't seem to be *her* strong suit either." Wally pulled at his lapels to straighten his jacket. His expression began to twist with his nagging memories, hands pulling more desperately. "What do you think it was about me that drove them away, Bud? Was I too small and too cute to be taken seriously, to be loved as a man and not some lapdog? Wasn't I witty or clever enough?"

Wally's voice quivered, sentences looping up at the end in helpless pleading. "Was it the depression? I was getting help, Bud, you know that. I was on the medication."

"Wally, don't do this to yourself. Other people have hang-ups too." When Marlon said it, hearing the words, he believed it; even if he'd never really believed it before. Now it made sense. A lot of things were starting to make sense.

"That's sweet of you to say, Bud. And I don't disagree. Still, I know I made a lot of mistakes, some of the same mistakes I was mad at other people for making."

Marlon knew what Wally meant. He approached holding an

imaginary whip. Wally turned, wrists crossed above his head as though tied there. Marlon cracked the whip, his voice even heavier with a feminine lisp than usual.

"Say my name, you little weasel, you worthless piece of slime!"

Wally whined, "Mistress Dominasia."

"Again, you pathetic toad!"

In the echoing crack of another kiss of the whip, Wally said, "Mistress Dominasia!"

"Nauseating pervert, again!"

"Mistress Dominasia!"

"That's better." The whip vanished from Marlon's empty hand as he approached Wally. Wally lowered his arms. In his own voice, Marlon said, "We all have our little hobbies."

"I'm not sure which I'd rather have people believe, the truth or the rumor." Marlon turned his head with new curiosity. "Y'know, about us. They've always whispered about it; back in New York, even on the school yard in Evanston."

Marlon reviewed the childhood images of games and horseplay, wrestling and roughhousing. "We were kids, Wally. That kind of playground bullshit doesn't mean anything."

"Except we're grownups now, and in a much muddier sandbox." Wally filled the snifter. "People you think are your friends become vicious, catty, even venomous. Y'know how they dealt with my death on *Hollywood Squares*? Producer went around to the writers' room and said, 'No more Wally Cox questions.' There's my legacy; 'No more Wally Cox questions.' When *you* die, they'll have plenty to talk about; acting legend, civil rights activist, land developer. But forever more I'll just be Marlon Brando's rumored lover, one-time star of TV's *Mr. Peepers*."

"Don't forget *Underdog,*" Marlon said, hoping the lightness of his tone would help elevate Wally's mood. "What's that he used to say?"

In the classic character's voice, so much like his own, Wally said, "Where're my residuals?"

In the familiar rhythm but in a gruff, mumbled voice more like Don Vito Corleone's than Wally Cox's, Marlon said, "There's no need to fear, Underdog is here! When there is trouble, I am not slow; it's up up up and away I go! Hey, sweet Polly Purebred, gimme some head."

As Wally chuckled, Marlon dropped the Vito Corleone impression to say, "Hey, Wally, remember the scene we did together in *Morituri,* that first one?"

"Funny you should ask." Wally took his place at one end of the room while Marlon started at the other. Wally stepped up to meet him, his voice wrapped in a nervous German accent. "Mister Kellar, Mr. Kellar!"

Marlon stopped as Wally caught up. "I'm sorry to trouble you, sir," Wally continued as the harried Dr. Umbach. "This trip is impossible for me, I'm not prepared for such a long sea voyage. I wonder if you could help me, perhaps? With your influence -- "

"I do not understand, Dr. Umbach," Marlon said, his own German accent more patient and resolved.

"I have to go back to Japan," Wally said, all sweaty twitches. "We have to turn about."

Marlon smiled and walked on, Wally's nervous doctor following. "You have an excellent sense of humor, Dr. Umbach."

"I know I sound like a madman, and I'm sorry to trouble you with all of this but, you see, I have certain ... problems. They are quite serious, I'm afraid."

Marlon, whose character was a civilian working covertly for the Allies to destroy the German ship, wasn't about to let this mousy, nervous doctor involve him in any complication. And he knew none of them would have the power to turn that ship around as it sailed out of Japanese waters.

Marlon's Mr. Kellar said, "What I suggest is that you jump overboard. At this time of year, the water will not be too cold. Depending on how fast you can swim you could make it back within a month or so." Marlon stepped out of the scene and back into his study. In his own voice, he asked, "Why was it funny that I should ask about that scene, Wally?"

Before Marlon could reach for the bottle, Wally said, "How fast can *you* swim, Bud?"

Marlon had almost forgotten how cunning and clever his childhood pal could be, and how full of life.

"So it isn't true then, Wally? You didn't -- ?"

"Kill myself? No, Bud, I would never have done that. I hadn't finished rigging Bill Armstrong's phone lines yet."

"Always with the phone company," Marlon said. "Forever tilting at windmills."

"I wasn't the only one, Bud. Of all the things we had in common ..."

Marlon thought about it and Wally seemed right again. He recognized the quixotic shades of his self-styled image and he was delighted. Marlon grabbed the ukulele and let his voice belt out the tune.

In the melody from the opening song of the Broadway smash *Man Of La Mancha*, Marlon sang, "I am I, Marlon Brando -- "

"Bud? Bud!" Marlon stopped singing to see Wally shaking his head. "Give me the ukulele, Bud."

Marlon clung to the little instrument. After a stern look from Wally, Marlon extended the ukulele and Wally took it.

But instead of setting it down, Wally started strumming, singing his own line as sidekick. "I*IIIII'mmmmm*m Wally, yes I*IIIII'mmm*m Wally, I'll follow Bud Bra*aaa*ndo 'ti*iiiii*l the end -- "

"Wally? Wally!" Wally stopped and turned to see Marlon wearing a very familiar, very stern expression. Marlon held out his empty hand and Wally clung to the ukulele as Marlon had only moments before. After a tense silence, Wally handed the ukulele back to Marlon.

"Anyway, the phone company's no windmill," Wally said, "but a real, live dragon that needs to be slain even if it is scale by scale. And that's not the only time I took on an enemy a lot bigger than I was."

"That *is* the best kind."

"It's the *only* kind." Wally let a silent moment pass, waiting for Marlon to swallow. "So what makes you think I wasn't murdered?"

Chapter Five

"I was booked for four weeks in Vegas. I did *Dufo*, some of my other routines. And the first night I bombed, absolutely died." Wally took a seat and looked into the mirror of the small but clean dressing room behind the stage, just minutes after the show.

"The boss comes into the dressing room." Wally nodded to Marlon, his cue to step back and ready his entrance in the role of Wally's boss. "You know this type of guy, booking the joints in Vegas."

"Connected."

"Right. He had a reputation Caligula would have envied. And he says -- "

"Look, Mr. Pepper," Marlon said in a gruff Bronx accent. "T'ings ain't workin out like we figured, know what I mean?"

"I do."

And Marlon also knew, even though he'd never heard the story. He sensed what would happen and how. What he couldn't figure out, Wally would surely indicate. Marlon's mafia booking agent said to Wally, "So, y'know, feel free to collect whatevers y'brought wicha's. See y'round, Poopers."

Marlon turned to walk away, ear ready for his cue. "Then I came back early the next day," Wally said, directing Marlon just as expected. "And the guy comes back into the dressing room, this time *before* the show.

And he brought the bouncer. A bouncer, by the way, is somebody who is too big to bounce a ball again in his life, ever."

Marlon's boss character said, "I dunno, maybe I don't talk so good. Or maybe you don't hear so good." He looked at his new, invisible henchman. "Maybe he don't remember so good."

Marlon turned back to Wally. "I'll put it in brainiac talk for ya's so's you'll get it. Your services will no longer be transpired. *Capice*?"

"I take it you'd rather I not finish my engagement?"

"Bada bing, bada boom!" Marlon turned back to his imagined bouncer, whose company he was fast coming to enjoy. "I knew the little *Eisenstein* would catch on."

"Of course, I do have a contract which specifies that the only condition under which I shall not be paid is if I fail to appear. As you can see, I have appeared."

Marlon could feel the imagined man behind him lurch forward, ready to extinguish this insulting little inconvenience once and for all. Marlon raised his hand to hold the man back. "Okay, Rocko, take it easy." Eyes still on Wally, Marlon's boss character said, "What if we's come to a new agreement? A verbal contract whereby you goes back to Hollywood forgoing all financial *oblongations*. And in turn, we let cha's go."

"And if not? Of course you've considered that I'm not merely some nameless transient who will disappear without a trace. Do you think your handlers really want that kind of complication to get in the way of their daily business?" Wally cleared his throat to add, "And by that I mean the fair and lawful running of this fine establishment."

Marlon's face was inches from Wally's, the tip of his nose almost pressing against Wally's cheek. Marlon's breath fogged his old friend's eyeglasses.

It was coming together in Marlon's mind; the series of mistakes Wally made, leading him straight to an early grave. "All right, four eyes, you'll get yours." Marlon reached into his breast pocket as he imagined this man might have done just two or so years before. He pulled out what Wally must have thought at first glance was a gun, but the light revealed a wad of bills. He peeled off two thousand dollars and dropped it on the makeup table.

"We'll be back," Marlon said, walking away to leave the place and time all together.

Wally's answer, "So will I," followed Marlon back to the study of the Brando house in the year nineteen-seventy-four. Wally added, "Four weeks later, we'd been through the same routine almost two dozen times. After picking up my last payment, I went home without ever doing a second show."

"Wally, that's *Bartleby the Scrivener*."

"Exactly," Wally said with a familiar ring. "A modern-day, heterosexual *Bartleby*."

Marlon took a careful, quiet step toward Wally, transporting them back to a different place, even if the time was not so far removed. Now they were in Wally's house on that fateful night. "But you'd insulted their honor," Marlon said. "And for them, you dying on stage wasn't enough. So after you thought the whole thing forgotten they came back, tracked you down to your cozy Bel-Air hideaway -- "

"I wasn't exactly hiding away," Wally said as Marlon pulled a cushion from the love seat, holding it flat in his clutching grip.

"You were asleep, probably drunk, when they crept into your room." Marlon got closer, raising the cushion.

"Bud, take it easy."

In that familiar Bronx accent, Marlon's boss said, "Payback time, Mr. Poppers," before forcing the cushion over Wally's face.

"No, Bud, stop!" Wally pushed Marlon's hand away, the cushion falling to the floor. "I was only kidding. The Vegas story is true, but the mob didn't come after me. It's kind of a neat idea though, isn't it?"

Mentality of a serial killer, Marlon mused once again. "So what happened, Wally? You were so young, not even fifty."

Wally picked up the bottle and stood. "This, for a start. I'd been drinking more in those last few years. And you know it's not easy to quit drinking. Booze makes everything seem so ... so *real*, y'know? Ultra-real. Seems that way, but in truth it blurs reality until you don't know where to stop, much less why. And you can forget about how."

Wally walked from one chair to another. "Pat was out of town, I couldn't find any adequate ... *company*. So I took a few sleeping pills, drank a bit too much. S'funny, my heart was weak but my arteries were strong. They were like granite! I pushed the whole thing too far, I guess; massive heart attack."

Wally stretched out slightly, the second chair his death bed. A chill ran up Marlon's spine. He could almost hear those last breaths wheeze out of his best friend's nostrils, that muscular chest receding once more before resting forever.

Marlon asked his next question slowly, not wanting the answer. "What was it like?"

"Hurt like hell," Wally said without anger, without bitterness. And with what almost sounded like tenderness, even mercy, he added, "But not for very long."

"You stupid, careless son-of-a-bitch."

Wally nodded, slumped in his chair. "You'll get no argument from me."

Marlon's anger receded to reveal his bare sadness. The ukulele was light and Marlon's knuckles clacked against it as he plucked out a *G minor* chord and sang in a halting, atempo rhythm, "I went down to St. James Infirmary, held my poor Wally's hand. He was stretched out on that long, white table; so cold, so sweet, so sad."

The ghosts of New Orleans seemed to gather around Marlon and Wally with the resurrection of the decades-old melody. Wally sang, "Let him go, let him go, God bless him."

Marlon joined him and in fractured, friendly thirds thcy sang, "Where ever he may be. He can look this whole wide world over, but he'll never find another friend like me."

Marlon kept dragging his meaty thumb across the nylon strings, picking out the chord in a stumbling *arpeggio* as Wally said, "Remember that chicken you loved so much, it died and your pop buried it? But you dug it up, so he buried it again. Same thing happened twice more."

Marlon did remember, the sight of that dirty, decaying bird still fresh in his mind. With each resurrection it was more decrepit; inflating from the gases, then bursting and withering in a sheet of wriggling maggots.

"It's not that I thought I could bring it back to life, Wally. My savior complex wasn't *that* far gone."

"Yet. But the fact remains, you couldn't let go."

"I wanted to be the one to bury it, not my old man! It was *my* chicken, I wanted to ... Did you know a dung beetle can push ten times its own weight in shit across miles of the Serengeti?"

"So could you." Wally returned to his line of questioning. "At my wake, you locked yourself up in my bedroom, wearing my pajamas."

Marlon was only slightly embarrassed at the memory of being curled up on Wally's bed in the very spot where he died; the cotton pajamas pulling at Marlon's armpits and groin and knees and elbows, buttons straining against his belly and chest.

"I just wanted to feel close to you again, Wally. I didn't care if they knew I was there or what they thought of it. All those people, they just got in the way. You were *my* friend, Wally, no one else's."

"You're still talking to my ashes."

"They're a lot smarter than some of the Hollywood big shots running around these days."

"Didn't Pat want you to disperse them?"

"I ... I can't do it, Wally. When I die, we'll be scattered together."

Wally shook his head, his voice low and steady. "As long as that's still a long time off. And I guess it's what you do between now and then that concerns me."

"Between now and then I'll make a fortune."

"But can you buy your son's happiness?"

"I can damn sure try! Tahiti is my children's future, their chance for lives outside of this hellhole. I won't let this town destroy them the way it destroyed me."

"But that's my point, Bud. You're not destroyed yet, not if you're willing to fight. What about your future, your happiness?"

Marlon stood and paced around the center table, pointing at Wally. "If you're trying to get inside my head, you're workin' the wrong angle. The defenses are too strong." Unraveling an imagined blueprint over the tabletop, Marlon's fingertip found the blueprint's center.

"I can get you in, but I can't guarantee you'll get out alive." Marlon's voice was low and grave, straight out of one of their favorite war pictures. "If you wanna get past the ego, you're gonna have to knock out these two guards here and get through this area, that's the imagination."

"Your happiness, your children's; don't you see they're intertwined?"

Marlon's finger traced the blue lines mapping the fortress of his psyche. "This is sobriety, it's closed for renovation. Through here is a straight shot to the ability to reason, but without sobriety that area is prone to flooding."

"Won't you come to grips with the things that are killing you before they start killing your kids?"

Marlon's brain began to pound, words and images banging against the inside walls of his skull. He pressed his fists to his forehead, pressure failing to hold back the raging pulse within. One fist lurched toward Wally, index finger pointing. "I won't have you using my children as weapons of rhetoric against me. I don't like that game!"

Wally was calm, Wally was steady. Wally was right. "I'm sorry to be so frank, Bud."

"Stop calling me that! We're not kids anymore."

"We all need a little help sometime."

And he'd asked for it, earlier that very night. But that was then and this was now, and Marlon didn't care to talk about it now. Now he cared to grab his drumsticks and play a rolling march on the center table.

"Bud, you said we weren't kids anymore, so stop carrying on like a spoiled brat!"

That was all Marlon needed to inspire his next indulgence, a loud chorus of atonal *la la la's* sung at the top of his lungs.

Wally's voice barely pierced the cacophony of Marlon's tantrum. "Bud, those who don't know their history are -- " But he didn't even bother going on. This wasn't the way to reach Marlon, Wally knew that. And he knew which *was* the way.

Wally could only hope that his best announcer's voice could pierce the clamor of Bud's amusical performance. "And it's the third quarter. The Miami Dolphins are up by two, but the Pittsburgh Steelers have yet to call in their secret weapon." From the recess in the drumming and singing, Wally realized he was getting through. To fan the cheers in Marlon's mind, Wally's announcer said, "Coach Wally Cox is consulting with the players." Wally huddled alone in an invisible circle, a crude portrayal of himself as the coach.

The huddle broke and Wally's announcer said, "Yes, they're sending Bruisin' Marlon Brando onto the field and the crowd goes wild!" Coach Wally Cox hi-fived Marlon as Bruisin' Brando ran onto their pretend football field, hands raised to his throngs of adoring fans. Marlon grabbed the ukulele, pinning it to the floor between his feet.

Wally said, "Facing Brando for the Dolphins is Rowdy Robinson Poopers, Brando's one-time roommate and longtime rival. And here's the hike."

With a few indecipherable grunts, Marlon hiked the ukulele between his legs, tossing it into the air behind himself. Marlon spun and caught his own hike. He turned the ukulele, neck poking under his armpit and the body resting in his elbow. Then he charged across the field toward Wally, who was both crouched and ready in the person of Marlon's adversary and simultaneously calling the shots as the announcer in an unseen booth.

Crowds cheered in their mutual imagination as Marlon ducked and steamrolled his way past the other players. "Brando comes charging down the field," Wally's announcer enthused, even if Marlon was only shuffling from side to side and knocking his opponents back in pantomime.

"Brando just misses Tarjenko." Marlon ducked to accommodate Wally's call, a first in sports history. "*Oof*, there goes Kennelworth with a sharp blow from Brando's massive right arm."

Marlon inched closer to Wally, every step in the study equaling five yards on what would have been the football field. And Wally could only crouch, watching as Marlon barreled toward him. "There's Poopers," he said, anticipating the tackle of a lifetime. "He's a sitting duck against this onslaught, ladies and gentlemen!"

As Marlon came within four feet of Wally his charge took on a distinctly forward momentum, no longer feigning progress as he bobbed from one side to another. Time seemed to accelerate with Marlon's lurching body, only inches from Wally's much smaller build.

But Wally was ready. With one foot on the chair he easily stepped up several feet above his own height, leapfrogging over Marlon. His feet landed with a clap on the wooden floor. "Incredible," Wally's announcer said as each man's character fulfilled his separate destiny. "Poopers jumps over Brando, who charges ahead to a touchdown!"

Marlon jumped up and down, raising his fists to the crowd that filled his mind's eyes and ears. But if Marlon wanted games, Wally would give him games; even if it dragged them thousands of miles south or to another continent.

"*Toro! Venga, toro*!" Wally let the Spanish accent roll off his tongue. When he repeated the challenge, Marlon turned with a glint in his eye. He stooped, hands to his temples with index fingers jutting out of his forehead like horns. Marlon charged with a bovine grunt. Wally flipped an unseen red cape in front of the charging Brando bull. He spun as Marlon passed.

Once Marlon recovered, Wally said, "*Toro, toro*," yet again. Marlon couldn't help himself. He charged, his heart pounding under the sheet of flab that covered his chest and belly. Marlon's lungs strained, his vision blurred. But in his ears the crowd cheered again, this time *mariachi* music whining and plucking behind them. Trumpets and guitars called Marlon to battle, Wally taunting him with calls of, "*Toro! Venga, toro*!"

Marlon charged again, his hands slipping from his temples and index fingers losing their rigidity. His heart cramped up, blood throbbing in his veins. His mouth was dry. Gasping breath dominated his eardrums, legs lumbering to deliver him to the nearest chair.

Wally stood, not a drop of sweat on his brow or a strained breath in his chest. "It's a lucky thing for you my *picadors* are on vacation."

Marlon fell into the chair chuckling, almost giddy. But his heart ached as it pumped blood to his cramping lungs. He needed time to regroup.

"You like animal stories, Wally?" A silent voice in the back of Marlon's ear warned him against the territory he was stumbling into. There were land mines here, this was not a place for games. "Back at Shattuck Military Academy there was this little cat, feral, sort of a dormitory mascot. We called it Tigger 'cause it was one of those orange tabbies, striped, looked like the tiger from *Winnie the Pooh*."

Marlon could still see Tigger's green eyes, the white chest and socks, her little patch of fat at the abdomen. He could almost hear her purr, one of the loudest in his experience. "Tigger had kittens while it was still early March, much too cold. So we took the cat and her litter in, set up a box in my room, bribed the floor captain to look the other way. We even named the kittens; Roo, Kanga, Piglet, in keeping with the *Pooh* theme."

Marlon felt transported back to Shattuck; snow on that stately campus, marble buildings and willow trees, uniformed young men in perfect formation.

Marlon said, "So one day I'm walking home, and in front of our building there was a pond that still hadn't de-thawed. And on that frozen pond lay one of the kittens, Kanga I think it was; legs splayed, a splattering of blood underneath it. The ice had broken a little and the blood ran into the cracks, forming these dark red lines like fingers reaching out across a white sheet."

It was like it was happening again right in front of his eyes; that furry lump on the ice, the nausea it inspired in Marlon's churning gut. "The pond wasn't so close to the dorm building, and I remember thinking that the kitten might have stumbled out of the opened window, but how could it have fallen so far?"

Marlon released a heavy sigh to gather his fortitude. "So I looked up at the building just as another kitten was falling past, over my head. I had no chance to catch it, Wally. I ..."

Marlon's words trailed off, eyes staring into that returned nightmare. "Its little arms were stretched out, eyes wide and black. It didn't scream, not a sound. Maybe the force of the fall pushed the air out of its lungs, I dunno. It was urinating though, a stream of yellow like a tail on a kite. It must have known what was coming, don't you think, to be so scared?"

Wally sat in horror, almost incapable of speech. "I suppose," was all he could muster.

"When it hit that ice, the crack of it; maybe it was just the ice, maybe its ribs busting on contact, I'm not sure, legs maybe. That sound, Wally, I swear I'll never forget it." Even then the wet crunch, the muted snap, made Marlon shiver. "I looked up at the open window and there was one of the cadets."

Marlon's memory was perfectly clear, his picture of this man's pronounced brow and pug nose was razor sharp. Marlon remembered his smile, bent and flush with gums and an idiot's laughter. "This ... this man, this creature, was just then throwing another kitten out the window. And the look on his face; the twisted glee of it, the horrible joy he derived ... I can't even explain it. I couldn't ..."

Marlon's tongue became confused, flabbergasted, anger clogging his brain, heart overflowing with frustrated rage. "Even now I can barely ..." Marlon's legs pushed him up and out of his chair, stomping through the snow and then up the stairs of the dormitory.

"By the time I got up to the room he'd tossed out the last of them and locked the window. That was the only thing keeping me from throwing him out there where he belonged. So I grabbed that degenerate son-of-a-bitch and started beating the crap out of him." Suddenly Marlon found himself throwing punches at this bygone villain, limp in his clutch.

Wally stepped into the role of one of Marlon's fellow cadets. As Marlon said, "They pulled me off him," Wally was there to do just that.

"You tried to save the kittens, Bud. It wasn't your fault."

Marlon's head began to spin, memories pelting him from all sides. "Since then it seems, I dunno, like all my life is just one kitten after another; wonderful blessings being tossed out a window. You, my kids, my women, the Indians, Tahiti; I can't save any of you."

"But can you save yourself? That's the first step toward saving anyone else."

Marlon waved him off with a gruff, "*Baahh*!"

"You're repeating your parents' behavior. And in turn you're passing that down to your children. You said you wanted to be the father that your father wasn't. But you've become precisely the father he was; worse, because you should know better."

Marlon had to chuckle, but it came out as an exasperated gasp. "Wally, if I thought I was anything like my old man, I'd put a bullet in my head. And this time, I mean it!"

"Then you better lock up the gun cabinet, and I mean *that*. The drinking, for example; your parents did it."

"Wally -- "

"You do it, and now Christian's doing it. It's a learned behavior, Bud. Look at my family; my mom drank, I drank. Your family's no different. Not your fault, but you've got to be aware of what you're doing to Christian and to yourself. If you're nursing a broken heart with liquor, I'll have company sooner than I expect."

Marlon said, "You think I better stop."

"Yes!"

Marlon sang, "What's that sound? Everybody look what's going do*oooooowwwww*n." But the only thing going down was Wally's hope of getting through to his old friend.

"And you have to stop avoiding the truth with these jokes and games," Wally said. "You're a man with responsibilities, but you carry on like a child; the same way your mother did, if you'll excuse my saying. What was it you used to call your folks?"

Marlon didn't have to reflect long to find the answer Wally was looking for. "*Unparentish.* But I was a kid -- "

"And now you let Christian smoke pot and drink in the house?"

Marlon's blood slowed to a guilty crawl. "It's safer than making him do it out there, where he could be arrested or in some kind of terrible accident."

"That's very *parentish* of you." Wally cupped his hands behind his back and started pacing, a pint-sized Clarence Darrow. "Your pop hounded you about your schoolwork, the same way you do Christian."

"Any father would do the same."

The phone rang, making Marlon's nerves twitch. Wally nodded, conceding the previous point. "Your dad was gone quite a bit during your youth -- "

"And as an actor, so am I; I get it."

"Your parents had affairs, so did you."

The phone rang again, Marlon's anxiety tightening the muscles of his back.

Wally said, "You felt your mother ignored you for her social life and for show business, and you ignore Christian for the same things."

Marlon's skin was clammy, sweat gathering on his neck. The bile in his stomach bubbled up in a hot acid stew. The phone rang again, causing an eruption. The juices splashed up toward the back of his throat.

"Follow the pattern, Bud. Look at the future you're helping to forge. What will Christian say about his father when you're gone? 'He was all right sometimes. But he was also a brutal, ugly, hateful man; abusive to his friends, mean spirited.' Anna isn't poisoning Christian's view of life, *you* are."

The phone rang again, one too many times for Marlon's quivering last nerve. The cord was little in his fists, the line taught as he pulled it out of the wall. A plastic shard leapt from the broken jack.

"What would you have me do, Wally?"

"Just make sure you're not the one throwing the kittens out the window. Follow the pattern to its logical conclusion. You hated your parents, you hate yourself. Now Christian and even baby Cheyenne are in danger of inheriting that pattern. They'll hate their parents the way you did. They'll hate themselves the way you do."

Marlon's heart lurched in his chest, teeth gnashing as he dropped the phone but held onto the cable. The phone clanged when it hit the wooden floor. Marlon twisted his hands, the cable wrapping around them. One yank pulled the cord tight.

Marlon advanced but Wally held his ground. "It's not too late to break the chain, Bud. And this is where it starts."

Marlon took a good look at the phone cord between his hands, quivering with rage. *Is this what I truly am?* Marlon had to ask himself. *Am I a lunatic waiting for provocation? Am I just an animal? Was Pop right all along?*

Marlon lowered his hands, the cord becoming slack between them as he let the loops fall away from his empty palms.

"Your parents let you down," Wally said. "They were unreliable, couldn't give you the kind of consistent love and support you needed."

Marlon was seated again, even though he didn't remember sitting. Wally was still up, walking around in a reprisal of his legal persona.

"Your Honor," Marlon said to an unseen judge above him and to his right. "My parents are not on trial here."

"You began to hate the things about yourself that reminded you most of them; your father's good looks, your mother's acting skills."

The crowd in the old southern courthouse gasped and murmured in near-Victorian shock. Marlon had to act as his own lawyer. "Objection, leading the witness."

"And these were your greatest assets, the things you resented and held the most in contempt. So you set about to destroy them *and yourself* if need be."

"Your honor," Marlon said, "counsel is making a mockery of these proceedings!"

"You even forwent personal hygiene and wallowed in domestic sloppiness. Or was that simply an effect of your much-lamented absentee parenting? Is that the kind of behavior you want your son to emulate?"

"I demand a mistrial!"

Wally continued to ignore Marlon's objections, staring him down while playing to the spectators' frenzy. "Yet they're all you have, these despised inheritances, the only way you can survive in the lavish style to which you've become accustomed. Isn't that true, Mr. Brando?"

"Yes," Marlon snapped back, "I'm a fucking actor, okay? And I do it for money! A man's gotta make a living."

"Is that what Stella Adler taught you? How is it, going to sleep every night knowing you've become everything you hated as a youth?"

"We all do it, Wally; it's called growing up."

"It's called selling out!" The crowd went wild, gossip and speculation boiling over.

Marlon wanted to scream at Wally, to shout him down with a litany of insults and denials. He wanted to raise every brilliant point and cite every arcane precedent and reverse his cunning conversationalist's serpentine logic.

Instead he gritted his teeth, looked Wally in the face and farted; long and loud and deep and rumbling, wet and bubbling, a protracted and odious declaration of rebellion.

Wally turned with a wince. Marlon waited him out, his gut filling with another gaseous response. As soon as Wally began to speak, an adult, dignified, "Very well, Bud, let's -- " Marlon let the second fart go, this one putting the first to shame. The shingles on the roof seemed to tremble.

Marlon grabbed the bottle and stood up just a little too quickly, the room swaying around him. "You don't know what the hell you're talking about, 'self-destructive.'" After a long pull straight from the bottle, Marlon added, "My body is a temple. And I still hate fucking *Rites Of Spring,* so *pfffft* to your theory right there."

An awkward silence followed, filling up the little study. "Is this what happened to us, Wally?"

"It's what happened to *you* that worries me, Bud; back in Evanston, perhaps before."

No, Marlon urged silently. *Don't.*

Marlon said, "Because you and I, let's face it, we had a falling out."

"Something that left deep scars on you, Bud, that touched off your sexual confusion and your hostility toward yourself and everyone else."

Shut up, shut up, shut up!

Marlon said, "First off, and this has been gnawin' at me; it wasn't that bum cattle deal with my old man, was it?"

"You always bragged about sleeping with your housekeeper, but Ermalene was molesting you."

Marlon's head and heart were awash in a strobe of moonlit faces and cold hands, trembling whimpers and whispered lies. His breath became short as it had been years before, night after night; nostrils cramping around her day's worth of body odor and pilfered gin. The feel of her stubble on his legs, only beginning to grow hair of their own, still made Marlon want to vomit.

"How was I supposed to know we'd lose our shirts?" Marlon barely managed to say. "He was still my old man, after all."

"Did *he* abuse you, Bud, the way he did your mother?"

"And it wasn't that redhead I banged in New York, was it? Talk about nasty vagina."

"You mean Deloris, you slept with Deloris too?" Wally turned away from his focus for just long enough. This was Marlon's chance. Wally recalled, "She had one of the most aware and gorgeously flesh-covered libidos in history."

"Then that wasn't Deloris." Marlon pressed his advance. "It wasn't that time I came to your party and spent the whole night sitting under the dining room table? I just didn't feel like talking to anyone."

"That was a panic attack, Bud. I'd never hold you responsible for that. Although I might for you ignoring what caused it."

"Panic, obviously." Marlon skimmed the pages of his book of memories, finding little else that might have caused their rift. These were the things of which he was most ashamed. "Well did we even have a falling out? Maybe I'm wrong, everything was just ducky."

Wally took a long, considered breath, releasing it slowly with one corner of his mouth tucked into his cheek. "I'm sorry to report that nothing was just ducky. Not only did we have a falling out, we had several. Sometimes it felt like our whole friendship was just a series of fights."

"Friendships go in cycles, Wally."

"You treated me like a plaything; the way you treat everybody, the way your parents treated you. They dressed you up as an actor, a soldier, to go out and live their lives for them."

Marlon set the bottle down with a loud thunk. "That's enough about my parents, Wally."

"But you were no toy soldier and neither were we, your friends and your family. I was no hamster, Bud, cute and little; no kitten to catch falling from a window."

"You arrogant, ungrateful cur," Marlon hissed through clenched teeth. "You wouldn't have been anything if it weren't for me."

"That didn't give you the right to belittle me for your amusement; so you could appear funnier, superior to the wit you so admired."

Marlon gave it some thought, seeing a reasonable compromise in a shared guilt. "I guess there was some one-upmanship between us. And like you said, it takes two."

"But when you couldn't beat me, you decided to own me. You were so possessive, rude to Pat and my other wives."

"They weren't good enough. I was protecting you."

"You were protecting your property. We were like a dog guarding a haystack. You didn't need me, but you damn sure weren't going to let anybody else near me either."

"But I *did* need you, Wally!"

"What about *my* needs?" Wally's tone became strained, higher pitched. "My feelings didn't matter to you, nobody's ever did. You tried to break up your own parents' marriage because that was your preference. The fact that other people's marriages were on the line didn't register with you at all, as long as you got what *or who* you wanted."

"I've spent my life helping other people!"

"Because it makes you feel good, Bud. Because it defines your self-image. What are the Indians but an excuse for you to indulge your messiah complex? What was I but another underdog for you to rally behind? I wasn't a friend, I was a favor." Marlon's skin percolated with goose bumps, mouth going dry as his tongue became like a slab of rubber.

"And what happened when I wasn't as fawning as the rest of your followers, when I refused to sit back and watch you belittling people for sport? What happened when I refused to let you use *me* for sport?"

Marlon remembered the little digs, the unwarranted and unprovoked cheap shots, pointing and laughing with people whose names he couldn't even recall. "You always held your own," Marlon said, wanting to remember little Wally the wit managing his way through any of Marlon's worst barbs.

Wally surmised, "You got bored, fidgety. So you left me to die."

Chapter Six

"No! Wally, I -- " Marlon grabbed the almost-empty *Courvoisier* bottle and took a few steps around the little room to stimulate circulation in his legs and in his brain. "I tried to keep you around. I got you work on *Morituri*."

"As a broken-down junkie. You did the same thing with *Child's Play*. I flew to New York from L. A. *for an audition* no less. I thought I *had* the part!" Wally took two steps, out of Marlon's study and into the office of *Child's Play* director Sydney Lumet. Wally would play himself in this little scenario and Marlon would play the famous director.

Sitting down, Wally introduced the scene with, "Sydney Lumet says -- "

"The part is an alcoholic schoolteacher," Marlon's Lumet said. "You used to play a schoolteacher on *Mr. Peepers,* and Marlon tells us you're an alcoholic; so you should be perfect for the role."

Wally stared Marlon down as each slipped back into his own persona. Marlon said, "But I did recommend you for the part. I was doing what little I could."

"You're not the healer Dodie was."

"I figured playing a role like that, maybe you'd take the hint. You said it yourself, you were overindulging. I tried to get you to A. A., I *begged* you. If you'd gone, you might actually be here now instead of just an annoying figment of my imagination."

"Your efforts to get me to rehabilitate myself sounded terrific with you slurring your words. But remember how frustrating it was when I wouldn't listen?" With Marlon's too-quick nod, Wally added, "Then you know how I feel now."

"Anyway, don't blame me if *Child's Play* didn't work out."

"But it *was* your fault, Bud, with your demands and your bluster, your ego and selfishness. Once they fired you, there was no reason to keep me around."

Marlon searched his heart for some guilt, some trace of the worry that had been hounding him all night, and for years before. But he felt only recrimination, scorn, contempt.

Marlon poked Wally's chest. "So you lost a job, a job I helped you get in the first place; a job you were lucky to get and probably couldn't have done if you'd managed to keep it."

Wally's face began to change. His once-piercing eyes were now shifty, his compact smile a rat's gnashing jaw.

"You're just like all of them," Marlon said, increasingly unable to recognize his old friend. "Everybody wants a free ride. I supported you, I protected you. I let you follow along on my dates in New York when you couldn't get any girls of your own. I protected you from bullies when we were kids. You never would have survived Evanston if it weren't for me; sickly, little Wally."

"I pretended to be sick," Wally said. The five short words filled the study with a rancid stink. Marlon thought about it for a moment, mouth ready to fashion the question but lungs failing to push enough air through the vocal chords. His mind was numbed, thoughts slipping away with this impossible truth.

Wally said, "I pretended to be sick when you came over to avoid playing with you. But my mother felt sorry for you. And she wanted me to have at least one friend, so -- "

"That's a lie!" Marlon's hands jutted forward, fingers clutching Wally's lapels and pulling him across the table, face up to him. His eyeglasses fell off and without them Wally seemed even more alien, less the friend of old and more the intruder he was now revealed to be.

"I *learned* to like you, Bud." Wally said, one hand on Marlon's arm and the other pushing up against Marlon's chest. "We were both outsiders, we liked to argue and improvise. But as the years went on you became harder to know, and I learned how *not* to like you again."

Marlon's right fist balled up, coming to a tense pause just behind his ear; elbow cocked and ready to launch it into Wally's face.

"Hurt a minimum of people, Bud."

In a voice he barely recognized, filled with phlegm and hatred, Marlon said, "I'm only gonna hurt *you,* Wally." His skin tingled, his lips pulled tight, panted breath pressed out between his gritted teeth.

But Wally looked up, eyes unafraid. "Go ahead, bully your way through this the way you did our friendship; the way you did through film shoots and families, marriages and love affairs. If this is the only way you can love then have at it, tough guy! You're more animal than man!"

"Shut up, shut up, shut up!"

Thinking it hadn't been enough. And *shouting it* hadn't been enough. Finally Marlon's body reacted from an instinct to survive, a shiver to send life-sustaining warmth to dying tissue; a reflex action.

A blow.

Marlon could have sworn he felt Wally's jaw shatter. But the second and third punches came so quickly that Marlon could not count the effect of each. Blood poured out of Wally's nose, gushing from his mouth, flecks landing on Marlon's chest and cheeks. Soon the punches were blurring in front of him, arm pumping back and forth until he had to exert an effort to stop it. Wally lay prostrate, the room tilting and turning with the increasing volume of the white noise in Marlon's ears.

Marlon screamed, "Look what you made me do! How could you say those things to me?"

"You needed to hear them." Wally's lisp was even more pronounced with the sheet of blood covering his tongue, teeth, lips and chin. "Because you can't change them until you understand."

"But I respected you!"

"It's not enough to have respect. You have to *show* respect."

Marlon's voice was a desperate howl. "I loved you, Wally!"

"It's not enough just to love, Bud. Love can be a destructive thing too. Just take a look."

And Marlon did look; at the bloodied face of his old friend, at his own fist hovering, anxious to deliver a frustrated judgment. He looked at a lifetime of brutality, thrust upon him and emanating from him, leaving a trail of broken teeth and promises. Marlon saw his own shadow on the wall; more ape than man, a savage without the intellect to know true civilization when it finally came.

Marlon knew himself in that moment as he never had and never wanted to, so fully and completely that to ever be able to forgive himself or grant himself any mercy would be impossible. Every mistake he ever made or would make, every lie he told himself or anyone else, every angry impulse either physical or psychological; they fell into place, chiseling his name in stone so big the whole world could see.

It had been his fault all along; the failed marriages and broken friendships, the lackluster films, the squandered efforts to help those in need. He fell short because he couldn't control himself or his appetites, because the only love he knew how to give or receive was painful love.

Destructive love.

And it was all he could teach his children. Marlon didn't dare to imagine what destruction their own twisted senses of love would wreak. Now he saw the life he'd made for them; it was no tropical paradise but a stone cell.

Wally fell out of Marlon's stunned grip as Marlon toppled back into his chair. The chill of recrimination receded to a creeping warmth crawling up Marlon's spine. Marlon's conscience began to rise in his gut. All his mistakes quickened in his lungs, breath becoming short.

He opened his mouth to tell Wally that he understood, that he was grateful for this last-minute rescue. He wanted to express his unworthiness. He wanted to promise he could make up for it and more. He wanted to describe the new Marlon, who could love without hating and give without taking. He wanted to see his old friend again, and hold him in an embrace that would properly thank him for all he'd done.

But he couldn't do any of those things.

All Marlon could do was cry. It pushed up from the center of his guts, boiling over from the green froth of his churning stomach and erupting past his lungs and heart. His face bent with the force of the emotional overflow. His brain crackled and shorted out, electrical current flooded. The tears pushed up past his nasal cavity and into his eyes, squeezing out from behind them to run down his contorted cheeks. His mouth opened, a silent question.

But his hand knew the answer, and it curled into a fist and assaulted the tabletop with such ferocity that the window panes seemed to quiver. Then the silence returned, as it always did.

"You're right," Marlon said. "I'm no better'n the old man. And *he* was right, I'm nothin' but a fucking animal."

Anger swelled in Marlon's chest, indignation and a martyr's fury. Marlon's legs pushed him up again and back to the writing table.

"Bud, stop!"

The gun rose to his chin as if pulling his hand along with it. "No such thing as natural causes, not for people like us."

Do it, the little voice said in the back of Marlon's ear. *Do it, you coward. Pull the trigger.*

Marlon recognized that voice now, harsh and cruel. It was his father's voice. And it was his own.

"What have I done? Wally, I didn't know ..." The words sounded feeble, muffled and pitiable as they tumbled out in Marlon's beguiled wheeze. "S'all my fault."

Wally held his hand out, effectual even from several feet away. "Bud, don't you see?"

"You said it yourself -- "

"What about your children? Learned behavior. Your mother tried to kill herself, now this. Follow the pattern, Bud. We all become our parents; and our children become us."

Marlon looked at the nickel plating on the gun, winking at him from the increasing distance as his hand sank away from his head. The gun seemed to smile at him, a heartless killer thirsty not only for his blood but for the blood of his entire line.

"My kids," Marlon muttered, nightmare visions spraying across his mind's eye like Christian's brains or even little Cheyenne's; across the walls, the ceiling, his own startled face and theirs.

"No guarantees," Wally said, his voice lacking the assurance Marlon only then realized he craved. "But the best chance they have is if you put that thing down. Now that you understand you can turn the tide. Learn from your mistakes, Bud, teach them by example. It's all for them."

The gun got heavier and began to sink faster, descending to waist level. Marlon's muscles relaxed to near paralysis, eyes blurring to soft white. His index finger remained tense, the last combatant in a war that could still be won or lost with a single shot.

There was no trace of the vicious beating on Wally's gentle smile. "Save yourself," Wally urged him. "It's the first step toward saving anyone else."

Marlon's tongue and vocal chords pulled and twisted to get his words out. "Do you think I can?"

"Just keep doin' your God-damned best."

Wally always knew just what to say. But the years and the pain and the shame and the love were too much, and Marlon could barely speak at all. His stomach settled with relief, his stirred bowels slowing. His heart resumed a steady beat. His brain crackled with impulses, whispers and screams that faded into a distant hum.

The gun finally toppled out of his hand and onto the floor. But soon Marlon's empty grip was filled with the familiar weight of his old friend's shoulder, his arms wrapping around that muscular, misshapen trunk. His eyes slammed shut, a blanket of darkness alive with blue orbs of remembered light. When he opened them and refocused, Wally stood there; by his side, where he'd been all along.

And Marlon knew just what to say. "Thank you, Wally."

"All in a day's work, *amigo*."

"No, I ... " Marlon's lips twisted into a grotesque frown, curling up at the tips by the sheer force of his will. "I wish you really knew how sorry I am, that we'd had this talk when it could have made a difference for us."

"It can still make a difference for you, Bud. I know it will. You were always smarter than me, quicker."

With a relieved chuckle, Marlon said, "Smarter? You were a genius. I'm merely brilliant."

When Wally turned a hot bubble burst in Marlon's gut. "You're not leaving, Wally?"

But Wally was already halfway to the door. With a glance at the urn, he said, "If I don't leave now, I never will."

"Then don't!" Marlon's words came fast and petulant, the words of a child.

Wally cocked his head. "Sorry, old friend; no more Wally Cox questions. Goodbye, Bud."

No, a voice in Marlon cried out. *It can't end like this. It can't end! Do something, anything!*

Marlon picked up the phone, his voice loud and theatrical. "Hello, police? Yes, my exotic pets store has just been robbed and the man is trying to get away ... How will you know him? He's the one with the monkey!" Marlon looked over with a panicky smile, but Wally was at the door, only a few steps away from being out of Marlon's life forever.

"Don't worry," Wally said, words slow and steady in his calming monotone. "The promise between us -- "

Before Wally could finish, Marlon joined in to say, "Will never be broke."

Wally shuffled to his exit.

"Wally," Marlon cried out. His old friend turned once more, still there for him. It was too far to walk and Marlon was too drunk to try, but he had strength enough to hold up his hand, thumb extended. "Thumbs?"

Wally raised his thumb. He said, "Thumbs," and they each pressed their thumb slightly forward and then to the side.

Marlon's gaze fell away as he considered the moment. When he looked back, Wally was gone.

Marlon knew he'd never see Wally again. He'd never hear that voice, never feel the warmth of his humor or his hug. *No,* Marlon's inner voice begged, *just a little more time, please! Get him back, bring him back!*

Marlon called, "Wally? Wally!" with increasing panic. His heart pumped faster, urgency heightened by the silence that was his call's only response. Marlon's eye caught an inspired opportunity, and he stumbled across the study to grab the ukulele.

Boldness making up for his lack of finesse, Marlon sang out, "Shake ha*aaaaa*nds with Mr. Jazz himself ..." But even his fingers seemed to know it was pointless, so they abandoned the tune.

Wally was gone.

Wally was dead.

Marlon said, "Wally?" It was less a call than a whispered plea.

The study began to spin again, a lopsided course that sent Marlon staggering for a chair.

Marlon's fingers crept over the light wood of the ukulele. His left hand craned around the little neck. His right thumb dragged over the strings, plucking out the *arpeggio*. His voice was ragged, throat sore and swollen. He pushed the notes out, words clinging to the saddened melody.

"No one could ever do it a*aaa*s ..." A heavy silence passed. With a tired breath, he sang, "My friend -- "

The knocks on the door, timid suggestions of knuckles meeting wood, sent a shiver of anticipation up Marlon's spine.

"Wally?"

"No, Dad. It's me, Christian."

Christian. Marlon repeated the name just to remind himself how lucky he was to still be able to do so. His skin crawled with the proximity of his intended demise, tears running relieved down his still-warm cheeks. Grateful breath spilled out of his mouth, heart beating stronger.

Now he had the second chance he longed for with Wally. Death would not stand in the way of Marlon Brando hugging his darling Christian and telling him everything he needed to say and everything the boy needed to hear. No mere law of the physical world would prevent this happy reunion, even as no words could describe it.

It's like laughing your head off and crying your eyes out at the same time, Wally had said.

Marlon could only marvel. *You're right again, Wally.*

From the darkness on the other side of the door, Christian asked, "Dad, can we talk a little bit?"

Marlon set the ukulele down. The hollow, wooden clack of the instrument against the tabletop was the only sound in the room until Marlon smiled and muttered, "Funny you should ask."

The end

Author's note

When Marlon Brando passed away in 2004, his and Wally Cox's ashes were scattered together at Brando's request.

Disclaimer

Last Tango With Marlon is a speculative dialogue based on the lives and friendship of Marlon Brando and Wally Cox. In the interests of accuracy, dialogue has been inspired whenever possible by actual published writings and interviews of Brando and Cox.

Excerpts from *The Trial Of Davy Crockett*, a novella by Fletcher Rhoden, available from Trafford Publishing

from Chapter Two

Castrillón ordered five of Duque's *soldados* to clear a small room in the battered chapel and set up two chairs and a table which had barely survived the siege. Castrillón did not know these *soldados* by name, although their faces were familiar. But from the time he assumed leadership of their command during the battle they stuck near him.

The church had been decapitated. The pockmarked outer walls struggled to rise to a suggestion of the roof, which now lay in massive chunks inside the chapel.

The walls between the smaller rooms were torn to the ground by the slabs of fallen roof. They rose no higher than eight feet in some areas, as low as three feet in others. Morning cast an uneven shadow over the ground. Sunlight streamed in beams through cracks and holes in the clay rubble and poured in from the collapsed roof above.

Castrillón frowned at the desolate adobe cove, still fresh with the reek of panic urine and vomit. *Is this where I will meet my fate?* he wondered. *Are these the ashes from which Castrillón is to be reborn?*

Crockett slipped on the blood-slicked floor, nearly pulling Castrillón down. One of Duque's *soldados* helped ease Crockett into a flimsy wooden chair. It barely supported his slumping weight, his head threatening to roll down his chest.

Crockett's flesh-burned back pressed into the splintered wood of the chair, and pain hissed out of his lips like steam. Castrillón could almost feel the searing of his skin, the prickling agony. He held his hand out to Crockett, knowing beyond his own reason that there was nothing he could do.

But he little realized that Crockett was not yet as helpless.

A spark flared in Crockett's eyes and in his hands as they jolted upward and found Castrillón's neck. Fingers dug into his skin, electric tension streaming from Crockett's heart directly into Castrillón's throat.

Duque's company already held their muskets and bayonets ready to kill. Castrillón had no desire to see this *Salvavidas* obliterated in a moment of blind, passionate gunfire. He wanted even less to be caught in that gunfire. His nerves tensed in memory of a death that occurred only in dreams. But now the dreams were reaching out into the daylight; set free and their prophecy fulfilled by Castrillón's own greed and carelessness.

Castrillón waved the *soldados* off. In the corner of his eye, he could see them step back, guns still pointed at captor and captive alike.

Crockett studied Castrillón in his grip; then the room and Duque's *soldados*. It seemed to Castrillón that Crockett's brain was functioning, however slowly. The rage that consumed him ebbed, falling away just as his fingers loosened their grip from Castrillón's throat.

Finally, Crockett let go of both.

Castrillón let go of the images of his own demise at precisely that instant, replaced by his panting and coughing. He wondered how long it would be before all parties would attack again, perhaps successfully.

"I'm sorry," Crockett said, his voice slogging through phlegm and dust.

Castrillón nodded and eased back, rubbing his neck as he stood and grabbed his rifle. "Can you hear me?" Castrillón asked in his most deliberate English. "*¿Hablais español*? Do you speak Spanish?"

Crockett shook his head.

In English, Castrillón asked, "Do you know what has happened to you?"

Crockett nodded, his head sinking heavily over his dirty bulk. His eyes locked on something behind Castrillón. Cautious of trickery, Castrillón backed away from Crockett and followed his line of sight.

A dismembered hand sat on the floor, the fingers curled in around the upturned palm. Its pink skin was covered with its own blood. The *soldados* had cleared the corpses out, but blood was still thick on the walls and floor, chunks of flesh remained scattered. With Crockett under the guard of Duque's *soldados*, Castrillón reached for the hand.

It was heavier than he expected, the veins trailing several inches and sticking to his sleeve. He tossed it over the jagged wall into one of the neighboring rooms.

"Wonder whose it was. Dickinson's maybe, or..." A cough ripped up Crockett's throat, tearing his words.

Castrillón raised his half-filled canteen, the water splashing with a hollow, metallic echo. Crockett eyed the canteen, his parched lips almost quivering. He took it eagerly, his head tipping back, eyes rolling into his head. Neck muscles rose under his grimy skin as his throat worked to suck out the last drop of water.

Crockett wiped his mouth on his sleeve and handed the canteen back to Castrillón. "*Muchas Gracias*."

"*Señor* Crockett." Santa Anna's voice captured their attention. Castrillón leveled his rifle at Crockett as the tall *generalissimo* entered, quickly saluting and returning his hand to the trigger. Duque's *soldados* did the same. "I see my safety is well tended to," Santa Anna said in English to Castrillón with a lazy salute. He looked back at Crockett and added, "*Encantado*. Are you comfortable, Colonel?"

Crockett looked up at Santa Anna but said nothing. Santa Anna huffed as if not surprised by Crockett's silent response. "The battle is over, *Sr. Crockett*. I hope there can be some dialogue between us."

Crockett looked at Santa Anna and sucked hard at his front teeth, smacking saliva in loud contempt. "*Tal vez otro dia*," Crockett said to Santa Anna's impressed smile.

"What other time than this? Can we share no mutual respect?"

Two *tenientes* entered, González and Herrera. González carried a burlap sack which like González himself was flimsy and thin, the filthy shell sagging with too little to hold. Herrera clutched a clear mallet decanter filled with pale red Sangria. His other set of fingers were strangling the stems of two crystal glasses with angular knops and faceted bowls.

Herrera, with his unending smile and anxious, toppling belly, Castrillón shrugged to himself in a fleeting moment of silent privacy. *No less transparent than the decanter*.

Herrera set the wine and glasses on the table, González unfolded the burlap to reveal several tortillas and strips of hardtack.

"These are the provisions I serve my own men," Santa Anna said to Crockett. "Some are near starving." Crockett's upper lip crested in a hateful sneer. Santa Anna held out his hand to the offerings and added, "*Por favor*, Colonel, in their honor?"

Crockett looked at the blockade of enemy surrounding him. Sunlight cut his face as the shadow slowly gave up its ground. His eyes darted into the furthest corners of the room and at the gaping hole that used to be a doorway.

But there was only one option left to Crockett and at long last he seemed to embrace it, however unwillingly. He grimaced and clutched his wounded side.

"Maybe some o' that wine," he said.

from Chapter Three

Crockett nearly spoke, but his opened mouth was his only reply. It seemed to Castrillón as if Crockett were choking on Santa Anna's cool determination. Santa Anna sneered and added, "What of your slaughter of the Creeks, *Sr. Crockett*? How merciful were you?"

Crockett's horror remained, but the direction of his disgust seemed to reverse. Crockett's hand was shaking as he reached for the wine glass.

He clutched its stem with his quivering fingers. It trembled in his sweating, greasy grip and tipped over, the remaining swallow spilling and soaking into the rotting wooden table.

"We shot them down like dogs." Crockett took a deep, quivering breath. "Put twenty balls into one squaw. She just sort of ... exploded."

Crockett seemed to have forgotten that either His Excellency or Castrillón or Duque's *soldados* were still in the room. He spoke in a low drone, narrating the scene as it must have recurred to his mind's eye in gruesome, minute detail. "We trapped them in a cabin, many as would fit. They made the most fearsome clatterin'; poundin' and scratchin' the walls. Some tried squeezin' out through the windows. We shot 'em where they were and then we..."

Crockett sucked hard on his teeth, scowling at the vision. "Then we set the cabin on fire, burned 'em alive. First came those terrified screams, the great billows of black smoke. Flames started to crackle..." Crockett's voice fluttered in his nervous throat, filling again with blood and regret. "Lord, how they screamed."

Crockett covered his mouth with his battered, filthy fingers. Santa Anna looked at Castrillón in the moments Crockett needed to take another deep, heavy breath.

Crockett said, "Next day we were looking for food. We found a cellar under the charred cabin, and lo it was filled with nice, ripe potatoes. But the grease from the burning Creeks dripped through the floorboards in such amounts as to nearly stew them 'taters as in a broth of fat meat." Crockett shook his head, eyes still staring off. "But we had *such* a hungerin'..."

His Excellency stepped toward Castrillón. "And so we add cannibalism to their list of atrocities," he said in their native Spanish.

Castrillón reflected on the frightened but determined faces of these rebels as he struck them down, their blood leaping onto his chest. He flashed on the women of Zacatecas and for reasons he could not understand on the orange cat skewered on the *soldado's* bayonet, blood running down the length of the rifle.

What about our atrocities? Castrillón asked himself.

Crockett's posture sank deeper into the wooden chair. It creaked with his weight, threatening to collapse.

"We were speaking of my march to Béxar," Santa Anna said to Crockett in his forced but impeccable English. "I was given an army which I was told exceeded twenty thousand, and there were barely one-tenth that many. We faced war for the first time against an enemy with a different tongue, from a different world than ours. We believed we marched to meet a race of giants, an army of legends from the pages of Dante. The mind, as you know, can be a powerful enemy when deceived."

Santa Anna smiled but was again overtaken by his army's mercurial feet. "We faced wolves and Indian attack. We drank water infested with animal carcasses. Pestilence, intrigue, suffering; a trail of bones marks our path here, *señor*."

"The bones of impressed men," Crockett said. "In my country's army, even in the Texian rebel army, we are either regular or militia. While the regular fights for advancement, for glory and career, he still fights of his own choosin'. And the militia, bless their souls, fight for love of land and home and country."

"Whose land and home?" Santa Anna asked, begging for an answer he long-since knew. "Whose country?"

"But they fight 'cause'n their own free wills. If the U. S. starts kidnapping young men from their homes or taverns, drafting their aid as you and the European despots do, half the folks'll flee north and rightly so, you mark my words."

"But among your volunteers," Santa Anna said, "many abandon their posts at the same whim which inspired their enlistment."

Crockett shrugged. "Not *that* many."

"No fighting force can survive such a lax regiment." Santa Anna pulled at his sleeve cuffs again, adjusting the coatee to his shoulders. "And I will not tolerate your accusation that my army is a tribe of slaves. They sacrificed no less willingly than the men of your command."

"I mean no dig at your *soldados*, Excellency. They put up a hell of a scrape. You should be right proud your arrival weren't no less ugly than your journey."

"*My* journey does not at this moment stand to end at the point of a bayonet."

A smile wriggled under Crockett's bruised cheeks when he said, "Not at this moment."

About the author

In 2008, Fletcher Rhoden directed the acclaimed premiere run of his stage play in two acts, *Last Tango With Marlon.* He went on to edit video footage for a dvd, now available (*www.fletcherrhoden.com/dvds*) for sale or rent. Rhoden earned his first feature 'story by' credit on the award-winning 2007 slasher *Stump the Band.* Fletcher Rhoden is an acclaimed author / illustrator (*The Trial Of Davy Crockett*, Trafford), produced playwright / director (*Soul Cancer*), festival veteran short subject writer / director (*The Christopher Walken Ecstatic Dance Academy*), creator of popular animated short subjects (*Rabbit In The Moon*) and children's programs (*Balloonzee*). Rhoden's animated short *A Gentle Reminder* was screened at Spike & Mike's Sick & Twisted Festival of Animation's famous "Gauntlet" at the San Diego Comicon, 2007, Rhoden is also a songwriter and performer (*I Love You, Now Change*), radio producer and personality (*The Mighty Three*), extended solo exhibition painter (*Fletcher Rhoden Sleeps With The Fishes*) and muralist (*Kenmore Island*). Rhoden has screenplays and unpublished novels and children's books available to producers and publishers.

www.ingramcontent.com/pod-product-compliance
Ingram Content Group UK Ltd.
Pitfield, Milton Keynes, MK11 3LW, UK
UKHW020136250726
13967UKWH00002B/681